fairytales for femmes

Vol. 2

L. Holm

Solibris Publishers

First edition 2018
Copyright © L.Holm
Cover illustration © L. Holm

Published by Solibris Publishers; Lund, Sweden
www.solibris-publishers.com

ISBN 978-91-978383-4-4
Printed by Lightning Source U.K, Ltd

Contents

The Illusion of Closeness

Kyra was in a chatty, exuberant mood as usual when she picked me up.

I have known her forever and she is my closest friend and I love her to bits and her charm and personality can lit up a small village in the North Pole. But she can really get on my nerves sometimes, especially when she is dressed to kill and insists that I accompany her to some shallow cocktail party. One glance at me was all it took.

"Morgan!" she exclaimed with the stamina of an opera singer, loud enough to make my comatose neighbor across the street drop his remote control: "*Dress shabbily and they remember the dress; dress impeccably and they remember the woman!*"

So she ransacked my wardrobe and found the little black Chanel she had bestowed on me a year ago that I had hidden under a pile of sweaters, and she forced me to change into the dress, opened her own makeup bag, ordered me close my eyes, sprayed on a cloud of expensive perfume, and performed some miracles with my face and hair, and twenty minutes later we were on our way to the party in her small car named Van Doris.

"Who knows, you might even have some fun tonight!" she said, slightly annoyed with my lack of enthusiasm.

"Well, finally I will get a glimpse at your handsome boss. And you just might get lucky tonight," I said.

"Well so do you, gorgeous!"

"No."

"Things were more fun before you discovered you were gay," said Kyra, sulking.

"Not for me," I said.

"You looked happier."

"Not in private."

Kyra turned her concentration back to driving and picking out the mood setting CD for our drive from her bag in the back seat.

2

"You looked so radiant when you started dating again and met…" she started but immediately interrupted herself.

"Sorry baby, I forgot, about…*her*…" she said in a gentle voice.

"It's ok," I said. "I can't."

She let me regress, mourn and soak in pain for two minutes and then she said:

"But still, there is no reason to turn into a nun is there? Everybody gets their heart broken. Just part of life—period."

"And '*what doesn't kill you only makes you stronger*' right?" I said.

"*Yes!*" she yelled and slammed her fists on the steering wheel.

"No. *Not* true! Maybe for you but not for people like me!"

Kyra frowned at me.

"No. I don't buy that! Listen carefully now! You know the woman I have been telling you about; the new accountant, Kitten; —I don't remember her real name—she will be there tonight, and she is *hot* and out and she's been single for a few weeks and she wants to have some fun—no strings attached—but she is fed up with always making the first move!"

"*And*?"

She sighed.

"I give up. You need to get laid, Morgan. You really do. And we both know it."

Even if I would never admit it, I knew she was right. I needed the illusion of closeness, if only for a night.

Kyra is an incredibly lousy driver by choice and habit—always determined to make an impression, especially on people she doesn't know—and this particular night she seemed determined to take the concept of multitasking while driving to a whole new level. But after a few wrong turns and some serious cursing from six people (me included), we arrived safely to the magnificent party in the magnificent mansion on Elm Street where her boss Mr. Fred Krueger—also supposedly magnificent—resided.

The house seemed to have exceeded even Kyra's wildest expectations so she just sighed *wow!*"

Van Doris looked embarrassed and uncouth among the shining Mercedes cars and BMW:s and Lexuses and Lamborghinis and Ferraris on the driveway, but maybe that was just a projection of my own surfacing inferiority complexes. A butler dressed in formal attire with white gloves and butler uniform opened the door and suddenly the sounds of human voices and laughter and bouncy jazz music filled the air. Kyra was so impressed she cursed.

But she must have spotted her boss somewhere in the lively crowd of exquisitely dressed people inside the mansion and decided to act ladylike for once, so she squeezed my arm and whispered: "*Some cocktail party, huh?*"

Kyra's co workers recognized her and came over to say hello and to check me out. Apparently she had said some really nice things about me and my irresistible sexiness because they looked a little confused when we shook hands;

"Morgan *who?...? That* Morgan?"

But then the butler served Champagne on a silver tray and everybody smiled and toasted and Kyra cracked some indecent jokes. A big man in his early sixties, impeccably dressed in an black suit and a red silk tie, came over and kissed Kyra's hand and dug his steel eyes into her soft brown sexy ones, and I realized that this must be her boss, Mr. Krueger, himself.

"Welcome my favourite female employee!"

"I bet you say that to all your favourite female employees!" said Kyra.

I could see why Kyra liked him. He seemed arrogant and self centred with a brutal streak about him. And Kyra—like a mountain climber who always wanted to explore uncharted territory, and the harder the challenge, the better!—had made it clear to me that she wanted to climb her Mount Boss—maybe for no other reasons than that somebody (Morgan) had told her she shouldn't because the stakes were too big.

When Mr. Krueger moved away from Kyra for a few seconds to welcome two other guests I whispered to her: "*Please don't!*"

"Dunno—I wouldn't mind a promotion and a pay raise and a twenty-carat diamond ring," she said in her mock sexy voice and fluttered her eyelashes. When she saw the expression of pure horror on my face she burst out laughing:

"I'm just kidding! You are so easily shocked and so naïve these days, Morgan!"

She shook her head in disbelief and gave me a big smile.

Maybe it was his long manicured nails or maybe the steel in his eyes, but I started to feel uncomfortable around Mr. Krueger. I decided to have a closer look at the art on the walls and see how many artists I could identify without checking the signatures first. I could recognize a Warhol, and a Miró, and two Georgia O'Keeffes, an early Lucien Freud, and two Picassos.

But the notion that such an insensitive brute as Mr. Krueger and the likes of him collected fine art solely for financial reasons— as an addition to their investment portfolios—and kept the invaluable treasures hidden away from poor but art loving people like myself, except at shallow parties like this one, made me feel so dispirited that I had to find a distraction. I went over to the large buffet in the middle of the room and put some seafood on a silver plate.

Then I tried to outstare a pink shrimp and her friend the green asparagus and they won and I ate them both so I won. Little triumph it brought me, though. There were some poorly executed oil portraits on the wall close to the buffet and I recalled that Kyra had told me that her boss had been married several times to wealthy women and that he enjoyed some kind of a reputation as a lady-killer.

Suddenly I caught a glimpse of Kyra trying to catch my attention from the other side of the room, where she was surrounded by a group of supremely elegant admirers of both sexes.

"*Shee is in the k-i-t-c-h-e-n. Go-go-go!* "mimicked Kyra with her eyes and mouth and pointed in the direction of the kitchen with her fork. I solemnly obeyed. I couldn't pretend not to get the message. Whatever embarrassment I might suffer in the kitchen would be nothing compared to the embarrassment of having to admit to Kyra that I hadn't dared to talk to a sexy woman who had told Kyra she wanted to have some fun.

The odds were definitely in my favour since I knew that I— thanks to Kyra and her magic makeup skills—looked good, on the outside at least. And I needed the illusion of closeness for a few hours. I wanted someone to touch my soul and my body and pretend to like me.

She was leaning over the kitchen sink with a glass of wine in her trembling hand and I was startled by how sad she looked. She was dressed in dark blue jeans and a black blouse and her long brown hair was hanging loose and tangled about her delicate shoulders. Even if Kyra might have had exaggerated some of her assets just a little—like muscle tone, height and exuberant sexiness—she was beautiful in a fresh, natural way. She was hyperventilating, and standing there all by herself in the spacious stainless steel kitchen she reminded me of a lovely wide-eyed deer; some helpless beautiful creature who had lost her way and ended up her, in this unfriendly zone. I realized we had at least one thing in common: We both thought the party sucked.

"Some affair, huh?" She said and her voice was soft and warm but filled with sadness.

"Yes" I said.

"I don't know why I even bothered to come," she said and I remembered that she had just split up with her girlfriend.

"That bad, is it?" I said.

"Yes. Times like these make me remember!" She looked me straight in the eye and her big brown eyes were intense. Someone like Kyra might interpret this intense, dark gaze as sexiness but it wasn't flirtatious or sexy—quite the opposite actually, which made it even sexier in an alluring but unintentional way—and suddenly my heart started to beat faster and I could hear the blood pulsing in my veins just because she was looking at me like that.

"I don't want to remember. And still..." she said.
I dared to move closer to her and her intense gaze and she sighed again.

"I came here because I actually *believed* that *things* ..." she started. "Believed that... *life*... could get back to ...*normal* again."

She turned away from my eyes. Ran her long fingers nervously through her tousled hair and then she looked at me again.

"Can you believe it? You know—I actually thought I could handle it."

"I know; parties can be rough," I said. "They remind you of... *things*."

I put my hand on her shoulder and gave it a reassuring squeeze. It was an extremely bold thing for someone like me to do, but this time I dared. I knew I had to. She needed my empathy and a comforting touch.

"I just miss her so much, miss what I never had, what could have been—but never was!" she explained.

"That's what friends are for," I said.

"I don't know about that," she said. "Some wounds never heal." She looked so sad that I didn't know what to do or say, so I just said the first thing that entered my mind. Something I had heard on Oprah a long time ago.

"*This too will pass!*" I said.

"Dumbest thing I've ever heard!" She said and her eyes flashed with sudden anger.

Then she looked at my hand as if it was a poisonous, disgusting insect that had landed on her shoulder, frowned and brushed it away. I turned red and stumbled out of the kitchen mortified, with my cheeks burning with humiliation.

My heart was beating violently. This was the first time I had tried to pick somebody up and I had failed miserably. And of course I knew why: *'This too will pass.'* What kind of a tragic pick up line was that! The worst ever! I was so out of touch with reality I had made a complete fool of myself.

When I entered the big library people were dancing to Roy Orbison's *Only the Lonely* and I remembered how somebody once told me that the Universe has a great sense of humor.

Kyra was dancing with a co-worker who had introduced himself as Ken, the amateur chef. Mr. Krueger was having a heated discussion with a fat man who looked like a smaller cloned version of himself and suddenly Mr. Krueger left the room very upset. I stood in the corner and tried to blend in with the wall paper and drapes and succeeded splendidly.

Kyra was popular with her great looks and the timing of a stand-up comedian. Ken the amateur chef whispered something in her ear and Kyra whispered something back and he exploded with laughter. I could tell Ken really liked her, and if he was smart enough to act a little coy and hard to get, Kyra might forget about her boss for a few hours and Ken might have a chance to enjoy her company in a more private space later.

I managed to look so invisible that someone bumped into me without them even noticing it, but I spilled sparkling wine all over my black Chanel dress. But since I didn't want to return to the kitchen with my bad pick up line still flashing in my mind like a huge billboard sign, and since all the downstairs bathrooms were occupied, I followed the corridor and went upstairs, into the dark.

I found a soft white towel in a luxurious pink marble bathroom close to the staircase and I managed to wipe off most of the wine from the dress.

Sitting there, bored, sad and lonely, my ears suddenly detected loud, upset voices from a room at the far end of the corridor. I recognized the sad voice of the woman in the kitchen and the steely voice of Mr. Krueger, and I couldn't resist the temptation of eavesdropping. So I tiptoed closer to the room and hid behind the door and listened to the voices inside.

"Why did you come?" he yelled.

"I came because of *her*..."

"If you want money you sure as hell have come to the wrong place," he said.

"That is not why!" she said. "I just imagined..."

"You do pick the time, don't you?" he yelled at the top of his voice. "What the fuck is *this*! Are you trying to intimidate me?"

"Don't you have any respect? And the date—doesn't that mean *anything* to you?" she said.

"Why should it? But I promise you this: If you do try something, anything— I'll make damn sure you'll live to regret it!"

The door flung open and the last moment I took a quick step back, but he was too upset to notice me hiding in the dark and he returned to the party downstairs. I could hear sobbing from inside the room and hesitated for a second. But I felt so sorry for her that instead of walking away I stepped inside the bedroom even though my heart was beating so fast I was afraid she might hear it.

She was sitting on the bed looking at a black and white photograph of a beautiful dark haired woman.

"Hello!" I said. What could she do? Make me feel lika an idiot? Too late. She looked up from the photograph.

"You again," she said. She didn't sound angry though, just stating a fact.

"Yes. Elvis hasn't left the building," I mumbled, red-faced.

"*Hm...?*" she said and gave me a strange look. Then she asked, suddenly apprehensive: "Did he send you to spy on me?"

"*No!*"

"Then—why are you here?"

"Someone bumped... I spilled some wine all over my dress and all the bathrooms downstairs were occupied. And then I heard some loud voices and..."

"Do you work for him?" she interrupted.

"No, but my friend works for him. She told me about you."

She was quiet for a while and then she said:

"I very much doubt that. Very few people know about me."

"Oh, I guess my friend is a little different. She makes it her business to know everything about everybody."

"Whatever," she said. Then she started to cry again. She was sobbing convulsively now. I sat down next to her on the bed and lend her the towel. She blew her nose.

"I screwed up big time. I shouldn't have come here. What's the point?" she said.

"I didn't want to come either. But now I'm glad I did," I said.

"Why?"

"I met you!"

"You are funny," she said. "And next you'll be telling me *this too will pass*?"

"No," I said.

"No?"

"I won't say it again! Promise! I never use the same quote twice in an evening."

She gave me a hesitant smile from behind her tears.

"So, come on! Give me another quote then. I am all ears. I might need one now."

"Sure?"

"You owe me a *good* one this time," she said. "I have listened to so much bullshit the last half hour it could last a lifetime and I need to hear something wise and profound for a change."

"Let me think!"

"Go ahead—think! It might do us both some good."

"Ok!" I said. "Here is one: '*Once you label me you negate me*'. It's Kierkegaard."

She turned her face away.

"*Kierkegaard*; that means *churchyard*, doesn't it?"

"Yes, but it's just a name!"

"How awful!" she sobbed. "And how true!" .

For some reason the name or the quote, or both, made her sad. I moved a little closer to her on the bed and she leaned on my shoulder. We sat like that for a long time. I wiped her cheeks with the towel and she didn't mind.

"I'm out of quotes. What about a hug?" I asked.

"You're sweet," she said. "You are nuts but you are sweet. Yes, I guess I really need a hug."

When I held her tight in my arms I noticed how thin she was and I could feel her ribs and small breasts under the shirt.

"I am Morgan by the way," I said, my ear touching the soft strands of her hair, my nose drawing in the sweet fragrance of her body.

"I am Kathryn," she said, her mouth somewhere close to my ear. The awkward situation made us both laugh and we looked into each other's eyes. There was a spot of mascara under her right eye and I carefully wiped it away and she opened her mouth just a little. Something happened in the air between us in that moment and the next moment we were kissing. I don't know how it happened—it just did. It was a tender kiss, two lips touching innocently at first but then suddenly it wasn't innocent any more

She pushed me away gently and looked at me as if as if she had woken up from a dream.

"Morgan," she said, silently, out of breath. "Listen, I am quite… vulnerable right now and *this*…"

"Sorry! I know there is a time for everything and this is not it, but your soul called out for mine, Kitten."

"Believe me—it's not you—it's this creepy place…"
I kissed her hand.

"Would you mind if we left?" she asked. "Right now?"

"I'm just going to tell my friend. She will be so pleased!"

"Why? Why does she want you to leave? Is it because of your *compulsive quoting* condition?"

"No! It's long past my bedtime, that's all," I said and smiled. We went downstairs. Mr. Krueger crossed the floor and came towards us with his arms outstretched.

"Are you leaving? So soon? You'll miss the fabulous fireworks and the *Grand Finale*," he said and exposed twenty white teeth in the brightest of smiles. It was hard to imagine that this was the man who had yelled at Kathryn less than thirty minutes ago.

"You know—you *could* visit her grave…!" She said, her voice breaking with emotion.

He moved closer to her and now his eyes were filled with hatred.

"This is *not* the time, *nor* the pl...!" he started.

"...after all it was *you* who put her there!" She was trembling severely now. He gave her a cold stare, laughed and said:

"Calm down, Princess! This is not an open audition for some lousy off off Broadway play!"

"You *bastard*!" she spat.

He flashed his white teeth in that horrible grin again and then he said, in a steely voice, filled with loathing:

"Kathryn, you and I both know I'm not the only bastard in this room!" Then he turned his back on her and started talking to the person standing next to him.

By now Kathryn was trembling so violently and had turned so pale that I feared that she would faint, so I held her close—and this time she didn't push me away.

On our way out we bumped into Kyra who was engaging in a conversation with an amazing looking woman dressed in slacks and a blazer, who was speaking in a loud confident voice. They were laughing and Kyra turned to me and waved me closer.

"Morgan! Finally! You've met Kitten, haven't you?"

"Yes!" I said and smiled to Kathryn.

"No! We haven't met!" insisted the tall, attractive woman standing next to Kyra. "I definitely would have remembered you,

Morgan!" She gave me a big smile and stretched out her hand:

"Hi! I'm Clarice Foster, a.k.a. Kitten," and she continued: "What do you know! This seems to be a yet another example of mistaken identities and hidden agendas!"

Kathryn and I exchanged confused looks and to my immense delight Kathryn—Kitten or no kitten—clinged to my arm and squeezed it in a slightly possessive manner.

"After the fireworks I, with the assistance of of some of my colleagues at the Bureau, intend to have a little chat with Mr. Krueger and sort a few things out. They will arrive any minute now," said Clarice.

"Is this about my mother, Special Agent?" Kathryn asked.

And now we could hear loud police sirens.

"Yes. Thanks to the invaluable assistance from Ms. Kyra Kenzo here we have been able to gather enough evidence to put Mr. Krueger behind bars for a very long time. I hope you didn't mind all the secrecy, Kyra?"

"It was quite a challenge! And I did get to nail the bastard, after all, didn't I!" said Kyra, raised her glass and winked her eye at me:

"Did *you* have a good time, Morgan?"

I smiled back at her: "Best party ever!"

Kathryn looked at me with a tired, melancholy expression in her big brown eyes.

"Can I sleep at your place tonight, Morgan? It's been such a rough day," she said. And then she added:

"Come to think of it; it's been a rough life."

"*Life is rough so you gotta be tough*," I said. "In the meantime, I'll be there, and I'll give you shelter from the storm."

And so we went to my place and she slept like a child in my arms the whole night. But the night after that we didn't get any sleep at all.

That was exactly one year ago today. Kyra, Kathryn and I live together now in the magnificent mansion on Elm Street that Kathryn inherited from her mother. We have a priceless collection of fine art, four kittens and five dogs, a trained chef and a live in FBI Special Agent. And yes, we are all very happy.

"*Why?*"
"*Because.*"

The End

The Perfect Match

The sales lady with short jet black hair, dressed in a slim black dress gave me a curious look as I entered the boutique. I staggered across the room all the way to the leather armchair in the middle of the floor, fell into it, and said:

"I need new clothes. *Desperately!*"

My voice was very faint, hardly audible.

"Yes," she said after a moment of silence. "I think I might be able to arrange that."

"It's either new clothes or a rope."

"I'd go for the clothes if I were you," she said. "A rope is too much of a statement. Far too far out."

"True… And I can't stand the sight of any more blood today, which rules out the knife."

My voice sounded as if it came from a place inside my ordinary voice; somewhere very dark and gloomy.

We were both silent for a while. Then she said:

"Some boutiques carry labels worth dying for but I prefer clothes worth living for. "

"So do I. Which means I must get something as far from this fashion statement as possible," I said, and added: "Sorry. I usually don't behave like this."

She gave my coffee and blood-stained blouse and skirt a quick, disapproving look and asked:

"What happened?"

I hesitated for an instant. I couldn't remember when I had last confided in anybody; least of all a complete stranger, but felt that she was entitled to some kind of explanation. Besides, she seemed genuinely interested and I desperately needed some kind of sympathy.

"I come straight from the coffee shop around the corner from here."

"*Um-hum…*? So I gather you didn't fancy their Java?"

She was not only beautiful and sympathetic, she was funny, too.

"Unfortunately, I wouldn't know," I said. "Before I went for coffee I had an appointment at the dentist. It was an emergency because I was in a lot of pain. And…"

"Yes?"

"…when the dentist started drilling on my right molar I realized that I had been given a local anesthetic on the left side of my mouth."

"*Ouch!*"

"So when I went for coffee afterwards, to try to calm down and stop shaking and bleeding, and get my act together, I drank my coffee with the left side of my mouth… to avoid… and well… the coffee was *very* hot … and I spilled coffee all over me."

She contemplated this for a few seconds and then she said:

"But how come you didn't notice the mistake right away at the dentist? When he inserted the needle into your gum, I mean?"

"I just didn't pay attention at first—not only because of the pain—but because I was in a state of shock of sorts."

"Anxious, were you? About the appointment?"

"Yes. Well, on my way to the dentist I realized that I had forgotten my mascot at my desk in the office."

"Your *mascot?*"

"Placebo, that's her name; just a little allusion to her magic powers."

I could tell she found it very hard not to joke about Placebo, the Magic Mascot. But she resisted the temptation, probably because she didn't know me well enough to tell how serious my relation with Placebo was.

"...and so I returned to the office and got Placebo, and on my way out back to the elevator I found out...."

I took a deep breath:

"It's my birthday today."

"But surely you must have suspected... something?" she said. "Or was it the thought of getting older that had you traumatized in some way in the first place?"

"No, no!" I said, and I couldn't help laughing. "My colleagues are taking me out later tonight, celebrating."

"Not for an Espresso, I hope? Sorry, please go on!"

"Well, on my way back to the elevator I just happened to overhear a conversation between some of my coworkers. They couldn't see me but I could hear them very clearly."

"*Oh?*"

"I thought they liked me, you see, or perhaps not exactly *liked* but respected me—well perhaps *respected* isn't the appropriate word, either—but at least appreciated all the late hours me taking care of everything and everybody and everybody's pets and plants and pills and parking tickets and correspondence with the authorities and the IRS and the police over the last five years."

"*And?*"

"Well, anyway, I found out that the word is that whoever "scores" with me, tonight, will receive a hundred dollar reward."

"Could have been less!"

"*Charity* is one of the words they used. Cheap isn't it?"

"Yes. Definitely. I bet you are worth at least $2000," she said.

"What?"

"Double that sum after I'm finished with you," she said and smiled again.

"Give me a minute will you? I think I just might have the right outfit for you!" She said.

When she disappeared I took the opportunity to look around inside the boutique for the first time since I had entered. It was very elegant, softly lit, with a few selected items displayed like artwork designed for worship, draped on mannequins sculptured in dark wood. They looked like primitive statues from a museum, stolen from an isolated island inhabited by peaceful people a century ago. Something Picasso might have found inspiring, too.

I found the entire place enchanting, perhaps because I found the lovely creature who worked there breathtaking. Then I happened to catch a glance of myself in the enormous mirror behind the armchair and my enthusiasm faded. I didn't like what I saw. Not that I wasn't breathtaking too—because I was, but in the wrong way—in the "*molested by a hurricane sweeping through a coffee shop*" sort of breath taking way. Suddenly I wondered why on earth had I told her almost everything about my day of endless humiliations? The woman was a perfect; why should she care? If it hadn't been for her kindness and those little jokes of hers that felt like balm on my bruised ego, I would have crawled back out in the street and cried. Looking around I suddenly realized why I might be the only customer. Who could afford to buy anything in a place like this with those astronomical price tags?

She returned with an armful of clothes made of soft black leather and smiled a lovely smile. I noticed that there was something about the way she moved and spoke and carried herself that suggested that she might have other interests in life besides selling exclusive clothes to millionaires. I got the feeling that she wasn't simply being kind or adding up her karma points but that she was actually enjoying herself in my company. She must be lonely in a huge place like this even though she was surrounded by beauty and mirrors, reflecting her own.

"Here you are, Porcelina!" she said.

(*"Porcelina"*?)

"I hope you aren't going to let those creeps anywhere near you tonight? Knowing what you now know about their sexist schemes?"

My head was spinning. It had been a long day.

"Well—I mustn't let them know I know."

"Definitely not. Out of the question," she said.

"Actually: I didn't tell you the whole story. I left out the worst part," I said.

"On a scale from zero to ten I thought this was quite bad. Is there really more to this"

"*Yes*! I found out what everybody except for me seem to have known for some time now; they are going to fire me—sometimes next week."

"*Noo*?"

"*Yes*! Somebody lusts after my job because for some obscure reason this person believes that it is both glamorous and easy, with a huge pay check attached to it, and apparently she has made my boss an offer he daren't, refuse."

"*Brutal*! I guess the scalding and bloodshed and the practical joke shrivel down to nothing compared to *that*."

"That's where it really hurts, actually; the way they are going to dispose of me as if I was some kind of a Worthless Insignificant Nobody."

I looked at the exciting clothes she was holding and now it suddenly dawned on me:

"*Shoot*! I suddenly realize I won't be able to aff… "

"Just try it on! Please! Just enjoy will you!"

It was not the kind of clothes I usually wore. Or believed I would ever wear. They were clothes for really cool people with cool lives and lots and lots of money and cool friends to match it.

And I tried on the black leather pants and vest and matching jacket, because at that point in time I always did what people told me to do. "*Open your mouth. Shut up. Spit. Swallow. Prepare of the balance sheet and income statement. Check the cash receipts and cash disbursements. Get dressed.*" Things like that.

She helped me with the zippers and tiny hooks and strings and tiny beads and the high heel boots. And I couldn't believe my eyes when I looked in the mirror.

"Is this really me?"

"Yes. I can spot an unpolished diamond in a million miles. And you do shine if I may say so. Even without makeup and your hair undone."

I certainly did shine.

"It's very..."

"*Sexy?* Yes. Definitely. It brings sexy to a completely new level, if you ask me, doesn't it? Those trousers and that vest were made for you. It would be a sin not to wear this tonight. They were made for tonight, and for your curves to let them shine. It is all so obvious and I think they love you for it."

And she gave me looks that made me blush for the first time. I could tell how much she loved her clothes by the way she kept looking at them, sighing, wanting to touch them. She made me feel very relaxed *and* breathless at the same time—I just couldn't decide what to call this new sensation I experienced.

"Keep them on tonight! You must do this for them!"

"I can't afford them!"

"Let's make a deal, then! You must promise me you won't take them off until I tell you to! You are the perfect match. You were made for each other. Oh, can't you see?"

She smiled again, that lovely smile that made her eyes lit up from within like small sensual fires.

"I guess that came out the wrong way! I'm Nova, by the way!" she said.

"Veronica."

"Promise me you have a great night, Veronica? Something those creeps will remember you by! Something that will haunt them in their dreams forever and ever and ever, ok!"

"How do you know you can trust me?"

"I don't."

"And what will the owner say? If she ever finds out?"

"As long as she gets her money's worth in the end she won't mind."

"But if I shouldn't return *you* would have to pay for the clothes?

"Well you do seem more than a little accident-prone, so I know I'm taking a heck of a risk here!"

We both laughed. It was so absurd and silly all of it and it felt good to laugh.

"I guess what you really need is a Birth Day, Veronica. A real *ReBirth Day*. The first in a series of wonderful birthdays. One to set all the upcoming birthday standards by," Nova said.

And then she touched me lightly on the shoulder and—because I could endure almost anything at that point; any form of abuse, physical and verbal and because she was so awfully, horribly kind to me, and so good looking too, and making me feel a little good looking and desirable too—I started to cry. Because this was too much; this was the kindest thing anyone had done to me since—*ever*!

"That bad, is it?"

"Worse. You have no idea."

"Please don't cry! People get fired everyday these days."

"They do? This was my first time. This week. Must be a horrible thing to be fired *every* day!"

I tried desperately to joke about it but it only made it worse.

"They survive and move on to better jobs. Except for the bad guys."

She handed me some Kleenex and I wiped my face and nose.

"So where are they taking you tonight? For the practical joke disguised as charity work?" Nova asked.

"We will meet at a Chinese restaurant and later we will go to a club called *the Lantern*."

"I know the place. It's ok—if you like that kind of a place."

"Do you?"

"No. Not particularly. But the DJ is ok."

"Before you leave you should put some makeup on. Please let me!

An hour later I arrived at the Chinese restaurant.

Most of my coworkers were there, enjoying the free meal and the familiar jokes and obscenities.

When I entered the restaurant and sat down at the table there was an awkward silence. This was the first time in the five years that I had worked with these people that they had ever asked me to go out with them.

At first they didn't even recognize me in my new outfit and with makeup on and in a new hairstyle. But they recognized my voice.

"Hi!" I said and looked around the table. Fifteen faces were staring back at me. I realized none of them liked me very much. I also realized that the feeling was mutual. For some reason this subtle display of genuine dislike came as a surprise to me.

"Holy shit! Didn't recognize you at first. What happened?" Stan didn't know whether to sound pleased or disappointed.

"Life happened. Why pretend?" I said. "What's your excuse? Ran into a van, Stan?"

I sat down and they gave me furtive glances and I didn't mind. I didn't care. I picked up a greasy plastic menu from the table next to where my coworkers were sitting.

"What are you guys having?"

"Don't worry *Vey-ro-nica*! We have ordered for you!" Sven

said.

"A bowl of lice?" I asked.

Sven didn't return my smile. But I didn't care anymore. It felt good to know that my sense of humor was intact despite five years of repression.

"How nice, guys! All this for me?"

"Well you are all fine and dressed up and in a sunny mood!" said Gwendolen Boreeng. "How was the dentist's appointment?"

"It's my birthday. "I said. "I am *celebrating*! So tell me: Where do *you* go on *your* birthdays, Gwendolen?"

"Your *birthday*! But why didn't you say so?"

"I just think I did."

As I sat there I was remembering fragments of the conversation I had overheard:

"What if she is getting you know... weird romantic ideas?"

"Doesn't matter—she is getting fired, remember?"

"Best thing is you get paid for this kind of charity and she will get sacked but leave with a smile between..."

"You must come with us to *the Lantern* later," said Ben.

"I know I must," I said. "Why spoil the pleasure for you guys?" That silenced him for a while. He looked as if he wondered where the aliens had taken the real Veronica and who on Earth I was.

"Don't forget to say thank you! Afterwards," Said Ben, and then he and Glen could hardly refrain from laughing.

I was pretending to drink the wine but didn't dare to since I didn't know if they had put something in it.

I was pretending to be having a good time but I wasn't.

I couldn't remember ever feeling such an intense sensation of loathing, ever before in my life.

I was thinking of Nova and cursing my own weird behavior earlier. She was beautiful, stylish and fun, kind and sweet, and probably in a relation with a kindred spirit in a perfect match of perfect bodies, souls and minds. I wasn't in any kind of relation, —if you didn't count my dysfunctional relation with Placebo the Magic Mascot which I refused to acknowledge even on my weirdest of weird days to my own reflection in the mirror. I got the impression that Nova might be gay but I had always found it very hard to tell these things. I couldn't even tell if I—Veronica— was gay but now for some reason I wished that we both were.

Across the table Mr. Ben Boreeng Sr. and Eve Adams were sitting pretending not to know each other intimately—acting polite in front of Mrs. Gwendolen Boreeng—celebrating something probably: a) someone (Eve/mistress) getting a new job and b) someone else (Veronica/me) losing the same job. I was surprised at how much I despised them and how angry I was.

I felt so angry I could actually taste blood—especially on the right side of my mouth—and most of all I was angry with myself, for wasting my life; for walking around with blindfolds;

for missing out on all the important things while paying attention to all the insignificant boring matter nobody else had the time or patience or guts or low self-esteem to pay any attention to, and therefore delegated to my overflowing desk.

They were having a good time and I wasn't.

But I was planning to.

I realized I really had something to celebrate. My new life.

We went to *the Lantern* and I wondered why I had never been invited. Or—rather—*why I had never even considered inviting myself?* As if certain things were not intended for people like me, whatever that meant.

The music was sexy and I didn't wait for anyone to ask me to dance. I just wanted to dance and so I decided to do so without waiting for someone to ask me to dance, as if I needed anybody's permission or company to dance.

Also, for some reason tonight, I couldn't stand the thought of any of them touching me or talking to me. Dancing with myself I was reminded of how much Nova loved these clothes and the way I made them look. I was lost in the music for a few wonderful minutes until I noticed that Ben, Glen, Sven and Stan were approaching me from across the dance floor.

Then there was a tap on my arm and as a *deus ex machina* the waitress shouted over the music:

"Telephone call for Ms. Veronica Dragonfly."

"It has to wait!" said Ben. "I am going to dance with this little nymph here."

"No, you are not! This is an emergency!" said the waitress. "Please let go of my arm, sir!"

"Who knows that you are here?" hollered Sven.

"*Who doesn't?*" *I thought.*

I went behind the bar and picked up the phone.

"*Hello?*"

"Meet me outside in five minutes!" said a voice I immediately recognized as Nova's.

"You? How did you know...?"

"You told me you were going to *the Lantern*, remember? I am taking a huge risk with you, lady, you know that? Lucky thing I know the bartender and that she owes me a favor."

(*"How did you know I **needed** you? That I was thinking about you? How did you know you were calling at the exact right moment, Nova?"*)

"Yes—But—*why*?" I said.

(*"Why me? Me—Veronica?"*)

"Why?"

"Yes: *Why*?"

"*Because*. Five minutes, ok?"

And she hung up.

"I have to leave. Bye!" I said.

Then I left.

Smiling.

∽

Nova was standing outside *the Lantern*. She had pulled down her jet black hair and arranged it in a spiky hairdo, and put on a pair of tight designers jeans and a black leather jacket with very little, if anything beneath, and a pair of Dr Martens boots, and once again she took my breath away—this time looking like the androgynous twin brother of the ultra feminine woman from the boutique.

The taxi stopped outside *All kinds of Wonderful*—the boutique, and I was ready to go inside the shop and change clothes, but instead Nova pulled out a key and opened a door in the building next to the boutique, and we went inside.

It was an old house; very old and respectable looking and we went upstairs. The nameplate on the door said *Tracey Kingston* and I recognized the name from somewhere.

"Why do you have a key to her apartment?"

"When I take care of the shop I live here. Taking care of the old ghosts."

"Are you sure we can go inside? What will the owner say if she finds out you've brought someone with you?"

She smiled.

"The *owner*? I'll take care of her. You have to take risks."

The place was neat. Long corridors with old wooden floors and oil paintings of nude women smiling invitingly, posing for me up on the walls. One of the women looked exactly like Nova. (Only naked.)

We walked past a few rooms with closed doors and ended up in the bedroom. The only piece of furniture was a big bed with fresh white linen sheets and down pillows and covers. Opposite the bed was a huge window overlooking the river. The full moon shining on us from the dark blue sky—matching the blue shade of the room—cast a long white stripe of white light over the brown floorboards. The room was simply gorgeous with its mix of dark blue and white colors. There were no books, no TV, no computer, just a big, big bed and a faint scent of lavender

"Oh, gosh, I love this room!" I said.

"Thank you!" she said, beaming.

"Your boss has excellent taste!" I said.

"Oh! Well, yes ... She... I guess it comes with the money," she said. "She can acquire anything she desires."

"She must like you very much if she trusts you with this apartment."

"Not necessarily."

"But she trusts you, doesn't she?"

"No, I'm not so sure about that, either."

"Then she must be very rich if she doesn't care. About her priceless possessions."

"Yes. Very. So rich she can't think straight."

"I am sure she is secretly in love with you." I said and felt sad. "She *must* be! How can she *not* be in love with you? And why does she have a big painting of you in the nude in the corridor?"

Nova gave me a strange look. Raised her left eyebrow.

"I am her front person. She is a very shy, highly sensitive person," she said.

"Are you with someone?" I asked. "Please be honest. I am not in the mood for any more practical jokes tonight."

"No. Not for some time now. I used to be in a relation and— well, after she left me I found it hard to trust anyone for a very long time."

"*She*? So you are gay?" I could hear how relieved I sounded.

"Of course!"

She laughed.

"Isn't it obvious? Aren't' you?" she said.

I blushed and started to tremble again.

"Actually—I don't know," I said. "Silly—I know!—but I really don't know!

"But you know these things! You just do! "

"I am not so sure—do people always know these things? Even

before they fall in love?"

"Well then—why are you here? Why did you come with me?" Nova said impatiently.

"Because you want the clothes back, don't you?"

"Yes, but…!" She sounded disappointed.

"Don't you trust me, Veronica?" she asked after a while. "No you don't, do you?"

I couldn't answer.

"Now you are embarrassed…!"

I still couldn't answer. My head was spinning.

"…and *silent*!" She added:

"Perhaps a cup of coffee would make you talk? Or a deceased dentist?"

Her efforts made me smile so I told her:

"I had to go through a hell; so that I could see—so that I could feel—*this*—so I could feel alive—feel *me, the real me*! You were so nice to me. It 's so confusing, all of this. And I'm so attracted to you. And so *confused*!"

"Confusion can be nice. It's definitely a sensation worth exploring, Ms. Dragonfly!"

"How about you? Do *you* trust *me*?" I asked. "*Despite*…"

"I just took a big chance with you."

"You did. Those clothes. They must be worth a fortune!"

"Actually I wasn't referring to the clothes."

"No?"

"No! I knew I was getting them back. Because I got the impression that you always do as you are told? Am I right or am I right?"

"Yes, you are right," I said and smiled.

"So. Do you always do as you are told?"

"Until today I always put everybody else's needs before my own. You know: *"Needs, what needs?"* I said. "And secretly—*subconsciously* I guess—I hoped they would like me just a little if I always said *yes*. But the opposite was true."

"That's a foreign concept for me not knowing what my needs are. I receive information from all sorts of secret, *internal* —hint, hint!—sources," she said and smiled a very sexy smile. Again.

So I blushed—again!—and said: "*With me you have nothing to fear but fear itself!*" And, yes, it sounded goofy and pompous and very silly. But she laughed so much she had to sit down on the bed.

"In that case I must ask you to please remove the clothes. They belong to me."

I stopped unbutton the leather vest.

"To *you*? *But...*?"

"Come here! Let's skip the talk! Let's find out if you are gay or not!"

❧

◟

Two days later I had coffee again. But this time I smiled. Not a drop fell on the lovely white sheets where my beloved was sleeping.

Gay, yes, very, very gay indeed. Just like me.

Yes.

◟The perfect match.◟
◟

The End
◟

Waste

The old man opens the door to his living room and I thread carefully through the relics of a life.
Evidence of erosion surrounds us.
Swim before my eyes, inside the yellow light, weightless waste products. Tiny particles of dust float around like unborn children in a parallel universe and I think:
"Why does everything have to be so complicated?"
I'm blinded for a second. Maybe my mind is playing tricks with me?

The old man's voice is as brittle as his old bones when he speaks:

"Please, have a seat, young lady. Anywhere you like, except in the nice leather armchair."

I look around. It's not a big room, but not small either. It's a living room that has turned it's back on itself and stopped pretending to be a living room.

"A dying room," I think, and then:

"Why do I get these strange thoughts?"

I can't tell *her* about all my strange thoughts lately. She thinks I'm severely disturbed—mentally deranged—or at least that's what she tells me when we fight. Maybe she is right. Maybe that is why we fight too often.

There are only two brown leather armchairs in the room so I wait for him to sit down in the one he was referring to as the *"nice one"*. To me they look identical and I wouldn't refer to anything in this room as *"nice"*.

A small table divide the space between us and I am grateful for the division of space but secretly wish it had been a glass wall. The notion of having the old man's used air entering my own lungs is so repulsive that I almost choke on it.

Another strange thought that I couldn't explain.

Perhaps it's just that I dislike him so much.

Perhaps it's the sight of the two appalling looking cookies on the plate on the table.

Or—perhaps it's just that I'm pregnant.

The room is so still I can feel how it absorbs energy from my young body like a dying organism. A clock somewhere in the room rips away minutes from my life, kills time, with my own consent, marking the passage of time in artificial heartbeats.

"*I am selling my flesh, by the seconds,*" I think.

"*Cheap*" she calls me and I guess she is right. As usual.

There is a small painting on the beige wall.

It reminds me of a map, written down in haste, handed over, and stuffed into a pocket, folded, forgotten, and suddenly retrieved. Cherished for some dumb, sentimental reason. Hung on the wall as a reminder of something? Straight black horizontal stripes on the grey surface mark the direction. A red blob apparently the final destination in the right corner.

"*Too late, now,*" I think and stare at the red blob.

It's so offensive that red blob.

I take out the notebook and pen from my purple bag, put them on my lap, straighten my back and my facial muscles responds immediately, viscerally, as a reminder of my days as a waitress, and produce a smile.

"Have you ever been in love, young lady?"

His question makes me wince; thrown out casually as if he was asking me about the new shopping mall, when the real purpose is to catch me off guard and probe a hole into my head to have a look at the mess inside.

"A 'coward afraid of commitments, terrified of letting anybody close'. That's what she calls me."

"Actually, I'm not certain," I say. "It depends on my mood."

"Or whom you ask," I think.

"Can you repeat, please!"

The old man puts his old hand to his old ear, impatiently.

"It depends on my mood," I repeat.

"What does?"

"It depends on my mood what the answer to your question will be!"

He grunts. Then he says:

"Life is nothing without love. Ask me."

"Why should I? You just told me," I think.

The old man is staring out in the air, the claws of his old

hand holding on to the armchair as if he doesn't trust reality. His grey wool trousers and jacket are in good quality. I wouldn't be surprised if he slept in them, too. There is an odour around him that is sickening. Maybe it's the smell of old age.

He must have sensed my repulsion.

"I wasn't born like this, you know," he tells me.

"Born like what? Old?" I think, absentmindedly.

"*Wealthy*!" he says, as if he had read my mind. "I wasn't born *wealthy*!"

He is upset. But I can't tell if he is upset at me or at his memories, only that his anger is as hard to neglect as his faint body odour. It has joined the dust particles and created a wall of soft and sickening resistance towards me.

"My parents were poor," he informs me.

"So are mine," I sigh, not because I give a shit about their sacrifices anymore, but because I have moved on with my life, as the old man should move on with his life. Or what's left of it.

"*Poor*!" he shouts at the top of his voice.

I jump in my chair and begin:

"I have read somewhere that the richest two percent of the world's adult population own…"

But I am immediately interrupted.

"I played the game of love. And I lost."

"You … lost?"

"*Her!*"

"I see."

"She was a plain girl. And she was poor. And she loved *me*. So of course I *despised* her!"
He makes an ugly grimace that adds fifteen extra wrinkles to his already wrinkled face.

"We all make mistakes," I say calmly, and realize I sound exactly like my aunt, whom I dislike almost as much as she dislikes me, because she makes it into a lifestyle denying, suppressing, that little "thing" we have in common in our blood, that little deviation from the norm they never make love songs about.

"She only made one mistake. She loved *me*," he says.
I give him a quick look; the sagging, thin, milky-white skin over his scull, covered with brown age spots, on his hands too, and I can't escape the anger, verging on rage that he exudes. The toxic pesticides of old age are leaking out from his old pores are attacking me, and I shudder and mutter between my lips:

"They say beauty is in the eye of the beholder."
But maybe he didn't hear me because he remains silent for a while.

He is pensive. And his old voice is subdued, almost inaudible, when he speaks again.

"She killed herself, you know."

"*Oh…?*"

"Last Wednesday."

"I'm sorry to hear that."

"Don't waste your life!" he says and he is suddenly agitated. "I want to tell the world: Don't waste your life!"

"*Bring in the news channels!*" I think.

"*Let's talk about waste.*"

But I need his money more than he needs my sarcasms. And therefore—too poor to follow his advice and leave this suffocating place—I simply nod.

"Yes, that is so true. One shouldn't waste one's life."

"Of course it's true! But maybe I shall start from the beginning," he says.

"*Please do and make me a millionaire,*" I think. "*Enter dinosaurs.*"

"I don't trust recording machines. Do you have your pen and paper ready?"

"Yes, sir!"

Yes, and incidentally I brought my small contemporary recording device just in case my mind should drift or I should fall asleep, but it's hidden under my notebook.

I press *record*.

"She was very beautiful," he says out of the blue.

"But didn't you just say that she wasn't?"

"Did I? But of course she was. Well, perhaps I forgot."

So I scribble down a few words like the attentive waitress I pretended to be until I started to forget that I wasn't, just pretending, because everybody else was pretending, until that day I was forced to remember and got fired. Sarcasm on my part had something to do with it. And my complete lack of desire for male flesh in general, and for *his* male flesh in particular, however well described and displayed.

This old man is obviously senile. It doesn't matter. I need the money for an abortion. Then I am going to need more money—a fortune actually—to get drunk, or high, for a year or two, or a preferably a decade.

"She had the body of an heiress... No! *Goddess*. Goddess, I mean."

"Divine!" I say, but with my own, not so sweet voice.

"I don't..." he says.

I glance at his old trousers and shaggy body and inhale a faint smell of urine.

"Don't have the body of a god? True. No, actually you don't," I nod, smiling to myself, and suddenly I remember her words.

"*Hatred disguised as humour.*"

That's what she called it, my dark sense of humour. "*Contempt for human weakness. Based on fear. Fear of intimacy.*"

"No… I don't… see how I could marry her," he says.

"*But…?*"

"I did it anyway."

I lift my pen from the notebook.

"So. Just for the record. When did you decide that you loved her enough to marry her?"

"Never! I *never* loved her enough!" he says, very upset.

"I see…"

He sinks back in is armchair and sighs:

"I think she loved me too much. But she was poor and she wasn't beautiful. And she loved me. So how could I have?"

Waitress—me— asks customer:

"Loved her, or married her?"

"*Yes! No!*"

He slips into memory land and remains there for a long time, making himself comfortable in there—or uncomfortable more likely, judging by his expresson—but immobile and silent, until I am starting to feel like his memories are suffocating me, and the only way to survive is to cut a passage through the polluted air with words, and I do; I confess:

"I am bored with beauty."

It just occurred to me that I'm bored with millions of things and beauty is only one of these things.

"Well, maybe you are just not beautiful? " he says. "I can't tell these things, anymore."

"Obviously not," I think.

Most people, male and female, find me attractive, so I really don't care.

"You are too good looking for your own good," She once said and at the time I agreed because it was true and I liked it. I know it's still true.

But I don't like it anymore

"With all due respect sir, I am here to take notes, and I don't see why my looks should matter…"

"It mattered to *her*," he said calmly, as if he is talking to the empty air between us.

"That's only because we live in a culture that is obsessed with superficial things like…"

"I was *blind*!" he cuts me.

"Blind…?"

"I had perfect 20/20 vision but I was blind. Now when I am technically blind I can see for the first time in my life."

"What a shame," I say. And I mean it. I think it's a shame to be both blind and senile and suffer from a body odour. With my own eating and sleeping and recreational habits I might end up there sooner than I think.

"What do you mean? *Shame*?" He asks and he sounds upset.

"What a shame that you couldn't see…"

"A *shame*? It was a *disgrace*! She was *pregnant*! And in those days…!"

"And you couldn't see that she was?"

"*No, no, no!*"

He is very upset now.

"So you had to marry her?"

"How could I have married her?" he shouts. "That was out of the question."

"Out of the question?"

"Impossible."

"Impossible?"

"Yes, you see, I forgot to ask her," he says.

He looks up at me with his blind eyes. And maybe it's because I realize that he can't see me that it feels like his blind eyes can reach far beyond what I permit. Venturing inside my head for a few seconds he obviously doesn't like the view and avoids my glances.

"Forgot to ask her?" I repeat like the echoing waitress I suddenly have turned in to again. But he is silent.

"Ask her *what*? Sir?"

He remains silent.

"Sir? Did you forget to ask her to marry you?"

I scribble something in my notebook. My right hand does. I have no idea what.

"Impossible!"

"So, what exactly did you forget to ask her, then? What question?"

He has disappeared inside himself again.

Then suddenly, out of the blue, he asks:

"Do you want it?"

I stare at him.

"Yes or no?" he insists.

"*It*?"

"*The cookie?*"

I look at the white plate with the two dry cookies on the table between us.

"Oh…? Thanks but no thanks!"

"But I did it anyway."

"Did…What?"

"What? What, what?" he repeats and beats his cane on the floor repeatedly. So impatient with me, the young woman opposite the table, wasting his precious time that he punishes the floor for her offences.

"What did you do anyway?" I ask impatiently, gaze at the cane, and add: "*Sir.*"

"Nothing important. Nothing! Don't you think I would have remembered if it was?"
He sulks in his big armchair like a little boy.
I'm emotionally drained by now.
I realize I don't like people. In fact I like them less and less.
I don't even like myself anymore. But then again, perhaps I never did.

This morning I found out I'm pregnant. I'm still in a state of chock.
I got drunk after our fight that night. Really, really drunk.
It never even occurred to me I could get pregnant. I was too drunk and upset with her insane ultimatums to care about anything. Or anyone, for that matter.
   Not even abut him, our best friend.
I can never tell her what I did to purge her from my soul and body.
What I did to punish myself for getting too involved.
Or what I have to do now.
I can never let her know that she was right about me.
   "*I can't love anyone. I'm incapable of loving.*"
But she knows. She knows me like nobody knows me. Better than I know myself.

She will find out. And *then*…when she does…

What then?

I look at the painting on the wall. After the final stop, the red blob on the map, what *then* is there? Without her?

Somewhere from a distance I hear the old man say:

"Life is not an easy game."

"Really?"

Irony is wasted on the old. Maybe because old age is the ultimate irony of life? Is this the reward? For being good? For playing by the rules? For enduring?

Ending up like him?

"No. Life is not an easy game," he tells me, matter of factly. "Only young people think so. Because they don't take anything seriously."

"Is that so? Imagine!" I mutter between my lips.

"Excuse me?" he has a new wrinkle above the bushy white eyebrows so I'm sure he heard what I said.

"I don't think so. Life can be very hard sometimes. And especially to young people, I imagine!" I suggest with my soft waitress voice.

He nods, vehemently.

"Yes. And you need the cookie," he says. "To survive."

"No offence, sir, but I truly believe there is a little more to life than cookies."

He snorts.

"Especially when you are young," I add absentmindedly. He snorts again and laughs to himself.

"I knew you would say that! I'm an excellent judge of people!"

"I bet you are," I mutter, between my teeth.

"Bet? Bet on what?"

"I bet that you are an excellent judge of people, sir," I reply, so loud I shout, actually. Unintentionally. The old man jerks in his armchair.

"Why do you say…? Why do you *shout* ..?"

"Because you yourself just said so."

"There was one person I never understood. Ever."

"Who?"

"The only person that mattered to me, at the time."

"I see…" I say. Actually—I don't.

"I was never home, that's all."

"In our society, traditionally, men are providers so they spend very little time at home…"

"I wasn't *home. Home*. Inside this body. *Home!*" he yells. He is so upset he is banging the cane on the floor again.

"*Oh*?"

"Does that make me a bad man?"

"Maybe you had a limited amount of time to reflect..."

"I reflected."

"Aha? So you ... *eh* ... reflected?"

"Me. Only me."

"Oh ..." I say, lost now.

"None of them were present."

"*Them...?*"

"Haven't you been listening? Haven't you been taking notes...? Why? I told you to!"

He is so upset he is trembling.

"Of course I have been listening, but.... *Them..?*"

"No! None of *them*! Only *me*!"

"Because you worked so much?"

"*None of them were present in my reflection.*"

"*Oh?*"

"That's why I can finally see now. Now when I'm blind. And I can see no me. In here. *Home.* Inside!"

He is upset. He beats his chest. And then he beats his forehead with his palm.

"I'm not home. Here. In me."

"*Oh.?*"

"Is that all you can say; "*oh*"?

"I'm sorry but I really don't understand!" I say.

"No you don't! Your lack of attention... and blindness ... such a waste of time... my time... so appalling!" he says.

"Hopefully you will grow out of it."

He pauses, and takes a deep breath:

"Then again, probably not."

"Senility will never be sexy, that's for sure," I think while I scribble something illegible in my notebook.

I clear my throat and say:

"This is all very confusing! I admit I'm lost."

He grunts.

"*Ha*! Lost?"

"Yes, I am lost."

He grunts again.

"It's either yes or no! Yes or no."

"Yes or no?" I repeat, still confused.

I have lost the thread but so has he. He has lost his patience with me a few times already and so have I with him. But unlike him, I can't afford to show my frustration.

The air is saturated with angry energy. It's all his angry energy. This is his house, and being inside his property my time is his property, and I can't afford to let my rage anywhere out of sight. I can't. I can't afford to lose another job, regardless of how insignificant the pay might be, and at least the old man isn't touching me.

"*Have your cookie! Yes or no!*" he yells at the top of his lungs.

"Yes, please," I say and straighten my back, but the smile has left my voice a long time ago.

"I had one."

"A *cookie*?"

My voice reveals exactly how tired I feel. But somehow I just don't care. He sounds tired too, and sighs:

"I didn't know until it was too late."

I can't think of anything to say.

"I lost them all when she killed herself!"

I still can't think of anything to say. I feel like I am locked inside a mental asylum for two the size of a closet.

"Life is nothing without love. She killed herself last Wednesday."

"Who? Your lady friend?"

"No! No! No! She died a long time ago."

My mind must still be functioning because I hear myself asking:

"Sorry: I mean your wife?"

"I don't know. She divorced me a long time ago!"

My mind is blank.

"Then *who*…?" I ask.

"My daughter. My little cookie. I never met her. Not *once*."

I can't speak. I look at him for he first time. Really look at him. He looks so strange. Not really ugly but pale and small and childlike and confused, like he wonders how he ended up in an old man's body in an old man's chair. Fragile. He looks surprised, afraid and then relieved.

"Have your cookie!" he tells me.

"Yes;"I say and just stare at scared little boy looking at me from inside the old man.

"*Love her!*"

"Yes."

He takes a look at me with is blind eyes, pokes around inside my head, and smiles for the first time.

"Thank you for coming."

Then his head falls down on his chest. And I realise that he is dead.

I cry when I leave the building an hour later. I don't know why. He was a self-centred old man, blind and rude and smelly, who forced me to waste my time and do things for him even after his death; call for an ambulance and tell people about his wasted life and about his wasted opportunities to love and be loved in return, before I am finally free to leave.

So why do I cry?

How can I cry over the life and death of a person I didn't know?

I open my purple bag and take out my cell phone and when she answers I tell her that I love her and that we are going to have a baby.

~

The End

A Dog Named Destiny

"Welcome to *Hotel Trouvaille*, Ms. Bland!" said the hotel manager. "Let me help you with your bags!" And when Amanda Bland—who was exhausted and car sick after the long bumpy flight and the long and even bumpier ride in the taxi afterwards—said: "*Thank you*" she felt more grateful than she had in years.

"We have managed to accommodate you in a nice, quiet room with a stunning view of the sea, Ms. Bland."

"*Perfect!*"

The first thing she noticed when she entered the room was how lovely it was with a huge balcony facing the vast turquoise sea and the cloudless sky, and she immediately felt safe. It had been a rough year and she had escaped and now she was here, alone

and safe in this tiny room. She wasn't a spontaneous person and had never been so, and coming here was definitely a spontaneous decision—by far the most spontaneus decision of her life.
She hadn't told anyone she was leaving, not even her daughters. But they would understand, even if they didn't.

Few people liked her.
Her so called friends would have wanted her to confide in them and share all the gruesome details about her marriage and the unavoidable, scandalous, juicy separation. They would have enjoyed observing her pain at a close range while secretly taking notes, and have a good story to share with their own friends over dinner. A good story is like a scarce and valuable commodity: It will get you very far but only if you don't give it away all of it all at once. Amanda didn't intend to give anything away. She intended to keep her story all to herself. Let them speculate.
Friends—like hers—are greatly overrated anyway.

Finally alone and finally free she had arrived to a place where nobody would be able to find her and tell her what to think, how to feel, how to act. And—the most important thing—prevent her from ever stealing the spotlight from anybody else, ever! This time she had learned her lesson and her lips were sealed.

She had never done anything like this before. She had no words to describe this feeling. Good or bad, she didn't know. The only thing she knew was that the feeling was new and unfamiliar.

Her tiny room had whitewashed walls and felt chaste like a cell in a medieval convent, with a massive four-poster oak bed and a large window providing her with a spectacular view of the beach and the sea. She opened the white drapes completely and suddenly the entire room was bathing in a brilliant glow.

She kicked off her shoes and lay down on the bed for a while and enjoyed the silence and the hot sun beaming on her face through the windows, all those rays of glory burning in vain like a private spotlight and she loved it, loved the futility of it.

Alone at last, with no obligations—just some old memories to confront. But she couldn't deal with the truth, not just yet, so she decided to postpone the pain and the story telling a little longer.

People were taking long leisurely walks along the beach. The sun was high in the sky. She put on her designer sunglasses to hide her sad eyes behind their brown shields of protective glass. Her legs were doughy white but she didn't care. Legs aren't the mirrors of your soul. Legs can't look sad—legs are just legs—just more or less strong, more or less attractive, more or less exposed.

After a delicious vegan lunch in the hotel restaurant she decided to take a long walk and explore the surroundings. It was an excuse to escape the ever present ever nagging feeling of toxic insects moving under her skin and in her guts, buzzing *Deal with us! Don't pretend you don't notice us, because we won't go away until you do!* Never before had she behaved like this; like a rebellious teenager. She desperately needed to confide in someone very soon—or she would probably get sick—and that someone was of course, herself. But later. Not now.

She put on a silly straw hat and her good sneakers and a dark blouse to cover her arms. And she packed a novel, and of course the expensive camera, some cookies and a bottle of mineral water, and—just in case—a fountain pen and the yellow notebook.

∼

She walked very fast and kept her eyes on the narrow path close to the beach. She wanted to silence the toxic insects under her skin and in her gut, and walking at a quick pace always did the trick. The surroundings were beautiful. More beautiful even than the photoshopped photos in the tourist brochures, which surprised her, being an amateur photographer herself. This boundless beauty was far more than she had expected (or paid for) and she eagerly drank it with her eyes an inhaled the scents like an undomesticated animal.

She followed the narrow path between the two old villages as it disappeared into wilderness through the wood and was relieved that she didn't have to run in to any other tourist this far away from the hotel and feel obliged to engage in some meaningless chitchat in the middle of nowhere.

The narrow path she was following gradually turned into a small rack that was being conquered and invaded by the emerald vegetation and still slippery and shiny from the rain earlier the same morning.

When she slipped on the wet grass and landed softly on her back, she was more surprised than harmed, and she smiled because it reminded her of some wild adventures of her childhood. She lay on her back and all of a sudden she started to laugh. She didn't know—nor care—*why* she laughed. She only knew that she didn't have to report the incident or her whereabouts to anyone and that was the only thing that mattered.

She stayed in her childlike position for a while and from her low vantage point she could observe some insects on the ground. Then, when she happened to turn her head and look in the opposite direction she caught a glimpse of the most beautiful scenery hidden behind the rich foliage.

She crawled through the tunnel of vegetation on all fours, and sat down and relaxed on the ground, surrounded by the massive green green tangles of old growth forests and tiny blue and purple flowers and the buzz of insects. The long walk in the blazing sun had made her thirsty and she realized that she had got some bruises and cuts after the fall, which she welcomed—physical pain always made her stay sharp and alert—so she had a sip of mineral water and wiped her face with her blouse.

Suddenly her ears detected the sound of female voices somewhere close. Driven by a strange curiosity she followed the sounds and crawled closer, careful not to make her own presence known, and then stopped abruptly.

Two women were making love on the beach.

A thin blanket separated their naked bodies from the hot sand and the entwined tree branches over their heads made up a green canopy over their heads. Their presence at this secret sacred place was almost impossible to discover except from the very spot where Amanda was hiding.

At first she got upset.

This was after all *her* sacred moment and she was entitled to some peace and not supposed to be reminded of sex wherever she went, especially now when she had escaped far away from the hotel and into the woods just to be alone, and she knew for sure that all the benevolent forces of the Universe would grant her some peace after all she had been through.

But she realized that her reaction was childish and unrational. If she hadn't accidentally happened to stumble upon it— and the women had been less loud—this secret sacred love spot would have been almost impossible to find.

They obviously believed they were alone, far from the hotel, and perfectly camouflaged in the secluded spot in this secret sacred place. They couldn't see her. And Amanda reminded herself —once again— that most people believe that making love is a beautiful thing.

The wind was blowing in her direction so she knew that from where she was kneeling she could observe the two of them without being observed herself and listen to them without being heard. Their presence was an integrated part of the fertile scenery; and while they were caressing each other's naked bodies they were themselves being caressed by the sun and by the wind, while the sea was moving rhythmically, softly, relentlessly in the background as it had been doing for millions of years.

Masterfully like two divine creatures, half human half gods, one blonde and the other one dark, the two godlike creatures were making passionate love, and although it was an act of love, it sounded more like a violent, magnificent wrestle; a power struggle with loud inhuman cries.

Amanda, kneeling and hidden behind the tree, grabbed her camera from her backpack, put on a telephoto lens, and started to take photos of the two women. She didn't know why she did it, just that she needed to preserve this moment forever and to catch the expression on their beautiful faces when they climaxed and the sophisticated movements, touches and kisses that led up to the moment; *la petite mort*, as the French calls it; the little death.

She was admiring them for a long time, fascinated in a way she couldn't understand, since she wasn't gay—and had accepted a long time ago that she wasn't heterosexual either—and then she slowly moved away from the spot, careful to avoid the low branches and careful not to make a sound, or break a twig, or let out a sigh. And then she sat down a bit further down on the beach in the shade under an old knotty tree, because she felt the need to write about her impressions in the yellow notebook. She put her pen to the empty page and started to write:

Arrived.

She stared at her accomplishment as in disbelief. One word. That's all. And she was already exhausted.

Sooner or later she would have to write down her recollections of the life she had left behind, and all the reasons why she fled, but not now. Later she would allow the toxic ants she felt crawling under her skin and in her guts to feast on her misery till there was nothing left to feed on. But not now. Not yet. Not here.

She felt very restless all of a sudden, but it wasn't the old pain insisting on being recognized. This was a new and unfamiliar sort of restlessness awakened from its Sleeping Beauty sleep by the two women making love.

The silence was soothing. She closed her eyes and realized that the beach was actually far from silent, because the wind was making constant little whispery noises playing in the sand and in the treetops, and the sea was calm but making rhythmically breathing, soothing sounds like the big heart or a lung of a giant organism. She could hear the noise of a motorboat far away and the cries of annoyed seabirds.

Her eyes caught sight of the two women again. Apparently they had left their secret sacred love cave and now they were walking away together and moving in her direction further down on the beach. To her surprise she noticed that they weren't showing any signs of affection like you might expect—like holding hands or walking very close to each other or even touching—but just talking casually, like two acquaintances walking on a windy beach together.

They both looked so lovely in their faded jeans, tousled hair and simple t-shirts that she found it painful to look at them. Instead she grabbed her novel from her backpack and tried to force herself to read, but soon realized that it was useless since she couldn't focus on the novel. Reluctantly she gave herself permission to continue to observe them and enjoy their beauty from a safe distance. They were sitting down now and discussing something and it was obvious they were disagreeing. The blond woman was making wild gestures with her hands as if she was explaining something and her mane of long strawberry blond hair was whipping her lovely face.

A small white dog of mixed breed came running through the sand towards Amanda. A very confident little thing, she noticed. The dog walked straight up to her, then stopped, tilted her head and demanded to be petted. Amanda was so taken by her charms and big brown eyes that she forgot to keep a check on the two women for a while. The little dog was happy and sat there with her and listened patiently when Amanda confided in her. Amanda gave her all the cookies she had saved for herself because she suspected that the skinny little stray was hungry, if not actually starving. Then suddenly somewhere close somebody was shouting and the little dog wagged her tail and ran away.

Amanda felt a stab of disappointment and sadder than she had felt in a very long time; so sad she had to fight back her tears. Her own strong reaction took her by surprise and she told herself that the reason why she suddenly felt so sad for being abandoned by a stray dog she had only meet ten minutes ago on a beach, must be that she was physically and mentally exhausted.

Then, after a brief moment the little stray returned again, and this time she was carrying something in her mouth which she dropped it in the sand in front of Amanda. But by then Amanda was so completely overcome by fatigue from the long day—and from the long year before that, and the dark decades before that—

that she couldn't keep her eyes open.

Amanda must have fallen asleep for a few minutes, or longer, and then woke up from her involontary power nap with a gasp. She had no clue how long she had been sleeping but knew she must return to the hotel and have something to eat, to regain her strength. So she started the long walk back to the hotel on her strong legs now adorned with cuts and bruises

An hour later when she was sitting at a table in the hotel restaurant she removed the lovely stone from her backpack and held it in her hand. It was perfect; white, smooth, just perfect. She kissed it discretely, put it on the table in front of her and continued to enjoy the fried eggplant and the Chevré, spinach and tomato salad and the sweet white wine in her glass. People sitting next to her were talking happily, discussing things, laughing. She tried to hear what they were saying but gave up. There was a man sitting alone in the restaurant a few tables away from her and she noticed his inquisitive glances. She hoped that she wasn't his type so she wouldn't have to talk to him. She didn't feel like exchanging pleasantries or engaging in a meaningless chat about the weather or the hotel. She always felt drained by small talk—or by unwanted sexual advances for that matter. But she didn't want to be rude either. She knew he was trying to get her attention and looking at her and smiling, but she pretended not to notice it. So she started pretending to be watching the sun set until she forgot that she was only pretending to enjoy it, because by then the spectacular beauty had taken her breath away and made her forget everything, inkluding herself, for an endless moment.

She took out the yellow notebook again because she felt the need to capture all the emotions that came over her and had accumulated over the day, and with a great effort she wrote down all the words that came tumbling into her mind.

Love. A dog.

Three words…

Progress…

She smiled to herself and finished her coffee, asked for the check and left the restaurant, feeling much stronger but infinitely sadder. On her way out she passed the two women she had observed making love on the beach earlier. They were sitting in the bar waiting to be seated at a clean table. She noticed that they still weren't holding hands or showing any signs of affection. A cold silence enveloped them, almost as if they didn't like each other. "*Or have been married for twenty years,*" she thought.

She started to wonder if she had just imagined the whole thing. Or maybe there was an identical couple somewhere in a parallel universe that sometimes merged with her own, and that the two women from that other parallel universe were very much in love and holding hands and looking into each other's eyes somehwere else right now. And Amanda had just happened to slip though a narrow tunnel between the two realms through a wormhole hidden in the wilderness, and witnessed the tenderness of the other identically looking couple for a short time, just as she was witnessing the feeling of cold indifference between these two women.

The soft breeze outside the restaurant felt nice against her face. She didn't feel lonely. Nobody knew her. She could be anyone. A nobody. She wanted to be alone. And she was more alone than she had ever been in he entire life.

No, she wasn't completely alone. Actually she had found a little friend who liked her so much that she had brought her a gift…

Amanda smiled and opened the backpack to touch the precious little stone and realized she must have left it on the table back at the restaurant when she had gotten distracted by the man who had tried to make eye contact with her. She halted her steps and hesitated. That stone was special. It was perfect. It was a gift from the sweet little dog. Maybe she was an incarnation of someone famous? *Sappho? Pythagoras?* Or maybe she was just a sweet little innocent soul with the most beautiful brown eyes and biggest heart.

Maybe. Amanda realized that she needed the stone and that she would be lost without it. It was just a stone of no value to anyone else, but it was a sacred gift and she would perish without it.

So she turned around and walked back to the restaurant. She was heading straight back to her old table when she discovered that the two women were sitting there now. She hesitated; planted a big smile on her face, took a deep breath and went over.

"Hello! So sorry for barging in on you like this, but I think I might have left a small white stone on the table a few minutes ago when I was sitting here."

She smiled and felt herself turning red. It felt awkward somehow to be standing so close to them, knowing far too much and yet so little about them. They looked up at her.

"No. No stone here. *See!*" said the blonde woman and made an angry, sweeping gesture with her hand so that Amanda could see for herself. Two glasses of wine, a bottle. No stone anywhere on the small table. And Amanda felt silly.

The other woman; the one with the short black hair, gave her lover a strange look but didn't say anything.

"Sorry to disturb you!" Amanda said. "Its just, that little stone…well *never mind*! It's so trivial really!"

"No! It's not trivial at all!" said the dark haired woman. "I'll ask the waiter if he took care of it. Promise!"

"Thanks! That's very kind of you!" said Amanda.

The blonde woman gave Amanda a cold stare—as if she was suspecting that Amanda had plotted this silly scheme in order to make a pass at her attractive lover.

"Will you be around for a few days? In case it turns up, *stoned* and ready for some serious *stone clubbing*?" said the dark haired woman. She laughed. It was a warm and friendly laugh that had an unfamiliar but very pleasant effect on Amanda.

"Oh, thanks! I just arrived here today, so *yes*; I guess I'll be around for a while!" she said.

Amanda felt embarrassed but she felt something else too; a new sensation she couldn't quite get her mind around. Bold? Bohemian? *Alive?*

Amanda used to collect stones when she was young. Young Amanda had planned grandiose things for her future, despite the deep insecurities she had tried so hard to overcome. Then came a time in her life when she realized that in order to survive she needed to be like everybody else. More than she needed to be different from everybody else.

So she stopped collecting stones and making silly plans.

And she got married to someone who told her he was quite remarkable and that Amanda was fortunate to have met him and she believed him and they had two daughters.

She believed him for many years and then one day she didn't.

Now she had arrived this place to collect the pieces of herself and try to find out what was left of her true self—if anything. There was really no reason to feel silly but she did.

On her way out she overheard a little girl asking her mother:

"What did that old lady say?"

"I don't know honey. I wasn't listening."

"Why did she ask about a *stone?*"

"I don't know honey. Maybe she is crazy."

"What's so special about that stone?"

"I don't know honey. Maybe it's a magic stone?"

When she returned to her hotel room she was determined not to meet her own reflection in the bathroom mirror but she did anyway, just in case. And she was relieved to discover that she didn't look old, and she didn't look crazy either; she actually looked quite fine—almost beautiful—with this new feverish glow on her skin. There was nothing wrong with her clothes and she was getting a nice tan and the long walk and the rest had done her a lot of good, but her eyes were sad. She smiled at her own reflection but her eyes didn't smile back.

*

"It's not a big loss. Just a small stone from a beach, nothing special, just a gift from a wonderful little stray dog with a big innocent heart with no one to look after her," she told herself.

But she felt so sad, so inexplicably sad all of a sudden, sitting all alone in a room which looked more like a monastic cell than a room at an exclusive hotel, with two unpacked suitcases and a million unsorted memories of loss…

"You can't escape life by running away from it," old Amanda-voice told her. *"Grow up! Go back!"*

There was no TV in the room. She had a stack of novels and a few spiritual books. It had helped her survive but not to feel happy.

She thought about the sweet little dog, all alone and coping all by herself in this wild landscape, relying on the kindness of strangers and she suddenly wished that the little dog had been there next to her in the room.

Somewhere in the building two women were having a heated argument. Loud female voices were shouting, screaming, and she heard doors slamming. The lovers? But there were other guests at the hotel who might quarrel, of course. The retired couple, and a few families and local residents visiting the charming restaurant.

Still she knew the feeling it was the two women arguing. But why? They seemed to have it all.

About half an hour later there was a knock on her door. Maybe it was a message from the reception? She put her ear to the door and said, "*Yes*"?

She could hear a female voice on the other side of the door, and decided to open. It could be important. Then she remembered that she hadn't told anybody where she was.

It was the dark haired woman from the restaurant. The funny, sexy one. And she was smiling, once again revealing a perfect row of strong white teeth. Amanda felt a rush of joy.

"Sorry to disturb you at such a late hour," said the woman. And then she made a perfect vocal imitation of Gollum in *Lord of the Rings.* "But I thought you might want your **prrrrecious** *stone* back?"

She slowly opened her fist, one finger at the time, and smiled. Amanda blushed and couldn't hide her joy:

"Oh! *Thank you*! How *nice* of you!" she exclaimed.

"You're welcome!" said the woman and there was a question in her eyes.

"It's just…" Amanda tried to explain. "You see: It's a *gift*! From a sweet little dog. Earlier today."

And she felt her eyes filling up with tears.

"*Silly woman!*" said old Amanda-voice. "*It's just a stone!*"

"Oh, you mean that white goofy little stray dog, running around all by herself on the beach?"

"Yes! *Her!*"

The woman threw a quick glance around the room and her eyes caught the pile of books and the open paper back novel on the bed.

"I am Maya, by the way!" she said and held out her hand.

"I'm Amanda!" said Amanda and took her hand, and when she felt Maya's strong hand in own hand she had to close her eyes for a brief wonderful moment. The physical sensation was the most sensual thing Amanda had experienced in a long time, but Maya needn't know this.

Properly introduced now, and on a first-name basis, Maya felt entitled to enter Amanda's room. And to her own surprise Amanda didn't mind the intrusion of her privacy. She had always hated the dominant streak of entitlement in her husband but she loved it in this beautiful stranger.

"I can see you are reading *Strangers*…! Oh, I love that book!" Maya exclaimed.

"You *do*? But…?"

"*But*?"

"I don't now…you don't look like…"

"Look like I can *read*?!"

"No! I didn't mean *read*…"

"Of course you didn't!" Maya said and laughed. "…'cause that would have been extremely rude!"

"I'm half way through and I just don't get it?"

"You aren't *supposed* to get it! Not until the big climax at the end! Hint, hint!"

Maya smiled an insinuating smile. And Amanda had to look away to avoid her direct gaze because she feared she might actually drown in Maya's hot eyes.

So Amanda cleared her throat and said: "I'm so grateful to the both of you! So by the way; where is your friend? Waiting downstairs?"

"*Waiting*? For *me*? Kimberly wanted to go to the nightclub tonight. We went clubbing last night and the night before that and, well; I don't feel like going there *again*. Same old, same old. So she went with some of her friends instead."

"Oh?"

"Well, Kimberly likes the attention and I don't. So here I am. Bringing *precious* to a damsel in distress in her bedroom late at night."

They both laughed. The visual image she was painting in Amanda's mind was funny.

"*Sméagol* meets Madame Bovary in *a room with a view*!" said Amanda.

She noticed that there was a spark of admiration in Maya's eyes. "*Reading. The perks of not clubbing every night! Or; of having a non existing sex life,*" Amanda thought.

"But tell me; where *did* you find the sto... *Prrrecious*, I mean!" she corrected herself. "On the floor?"

"No. Actually it was *ten feet tall deep down* in a *rabbit hole*...! Just kidding. I'll tell you later!"

"I am so grateful to both of you! I hope your friend is having a good time with her other... friends."

"We're a couple, you know," Maya said, serious all of a sudden.

"Lovers," she added.

"Oh! *I see*," said Amanda and pretended to be surprised. "I didn't know. Must say you are very… *discreet*."

A white lie. But she couldn't possibly tell Maya she had been spying on the two of them making love a few hours earlier the same day. You can't tell people those things. (No matter how much you would like to see their reaction.)

"We try to be discreet," said Maya. "No actually that's not true. I am the one trying to be discreet. Kimberly hates it. She is open. She welcomes confrontation."

"Well, the world can be a merciless place sometimes. If you're not careful, I mean!" said Amanda.

"Kimberly likes to provoke people and force them to show their "true colors", or "cut the crap", as she puts it. She wants to fight the world, the establishment, me; all the time. We had a horrible fight earlier; I hope we weren't too loud. It's embarrassing. There are kids in the building."

Amanda didn't reply.

"Wow, you've got the perfect view of the sea!" said Maya and looked across the room out the window. "This must be the best view in the entire building!"

"Yes, it's lovely."

"Our room is not as lovely as yours. It is bigger but we don't have this spectacular view."

"I guess I was lucky."

"Yes, sometimes all it takes is a little… *luck*!" said Maya and gave her a sly smile.

"So, what are your plans for tomorrow?" she continued. "We are going on a picnic. Kimberly, myself and two of her friends. You are welcome to join us!"

"Well I don't know…"

"We'll rent a car and drive somewhere. Somewhere nice."

"But…"

But Maya didn't take no for an answer.

"Perfect! See you at eight o' clock tomorrow morning then!" said Maya and left with a big smile on her lips.

Amanda immediately regretted having accepting the invitation. Why on earth would she go on a picnic with Maya and her lover? It made absolutely no sense whatsoever. She felt extremely uncomfortable around Kimberly—because Amanda didn't like her at all and she knew that the feeling was mutual—and she felt equally, if not more, uncomfortable around Maya—but only because Amanda liked *her* too much and realized that the feeling wasn't mutual.

She was going on a picnic with four women she didn't know when she had paid a fortune just to get away from people she didn't know who pretended to be her friends. When what she needed most of all was just to be left alone and lick her wounds.

"*No you don't,*" the new Amanda-voice told her. "*It is just an excuse for not having to feel exposed. These people don't know you. You don't have to tell them anything about yourself.*"

"*But I blush!*" Amanda told new Amanda-voice.

"*Who cares if you blush?*" replied new Amanda-voice.

"But I care," said Amanda. "A lot!"

"Who cares if you care? A lot?" said new Amanda-voice. "Nobody in the entire world gives a shit about you or your feelings! Haven't you your learned that by now?"

"This is insane!" said Amanda. "I must end this conversation."
What would she wear?
She knew she looked great in her black slim jeans. She had lost a lot of weight these last few months and thanks to her reluctance to throw away things she had once loved, she had found a stack of old jeans from when she was a lot younger and a lot thinner—and a lot happier—that suddenly fit perfectly. Her sweet daughters had told her that the pair of old Levis made her look much younger and much cooler, and the soft feel of her daughter's kindness and the sensation of the *before-everything-jeans* caressing her legs, made her feel great.

She had a rough night. Every night she was assaulted by old nightmares and she always woke up sweating with her heart pounding frantically. Her doctor had prescribed some antidepressants but in the end she had decided not to take them. She just had to get past this time of her life somehow. Everything will pass if you give it time. Everything. Especially life.

When the alarm rang at first she had no idea where she was. She looked around the room and blinked a few times. Then she relaxed. And then she remembered. She had ran away from home like a scared teenager and now she was going on a picnic with a group of complete strangers; some women she didn't know and didn't particularly wish to get to know either.

Maya, the beautiful, sensual woman with the persuasive powers of a magician, had asked her to join them, out of pity probably, or maybe out of boredom, or perhaps because she just wanted some distraction after the horrible fight with her gorgeous lover. But it is hard to say no to people who are as nice as Maya or possess such hypnotic eyes. And she couldn't deny Maya the satisfaction of being a nice person, even if it would be at Amanda's expense in the end—as always.

She could tell she had turned into a cynical woman. *Boring* he had called her. *Cold and boring.* When they had met many yeas ago Amanda had been the one with the grand visions and uncurbed enthusiasm. Now she was drained of joy, optimism, lust, anything.

She had escaped her old life so that she wouldn't have to do or say or feel anything she didn't want to do or say or feel, nor conform to anyone's low expectations of her anymore; so how was it possible that not even here, among complete strangers did she get to have the last say in this matter?

"*Fuck!*" she didn't really want to go on a picnic with a group of young beautiful women, who probably had known each other for years and who would probably talk about Amanda afterwards, behind her back and pity her.

"*So go on; sit here all by yourself and feel sad and sorry for yourself,*" new Amanda-voice told her.

"*Shut up!*" she told the new Amanda-voice but for no good.

"You might even have some fun, you know," said new Amanda-voice. *"Some people actually have FUN, remember the word? FUN! No? Google it! And some people have SEX, remember! SEX! Especially people who don't sit around feeling sorry for themselves all day long."*

An hour later there was a knock at the door. She opened and smiled, determined to appear cool and easygoing and not being pitied.

"Morning Maya!"

"Morning 'Manda! Are you ready, *prrrrecious* stone lady?"

Maya gave Amanda another one of her high voltage smiles.

"Yes. You bet!"

For some reason Amanda blushed. Maya always had that effect on her. But Maya didn't seem to mind the effect she had on Amanda.

Twenty minutes later they joined the three other women waiting outside the hotel.

"Hello! I'm Amanda!" said Amanda, trying sound normal.

The three women standing next to the blue rental car stared indifferently at her. Felicia and Greta were young and tanned and almost as impossibly attractive as Kimberly and Maya.

For some reason Kimberly was sulking and barely had the energy to say *"Hi"* and almot accusingly add: *"We've already met"*. Felicia and Greta looked hung over with dark circles under their eyes and gave her a few additional strange looks before they reluctantly returned the *"Hello"*.

Amanda climbed into the backseat and looked out of the window. "*Maybe this wasn't such a brilliant idea after all!*" informed old Amanda-voice. "*Well, who knows, maybe it IS!*" said new Amanda-voice.

They stopped at a small grocery store to buy some wine and bread and cheese and fruit and cigarettes. Greta was dissuaded by the others to buy the cute kitten that was for sale next to the pots, vegetables and cheep jewelry, and she sulked for a long time afterwards. "*Fascists!*" she called them and started to cry.

"*Maybe blushing isn't such a big thing, after all!*" Amanda thought.

As the tension between Maya and Kimberly in the front seat was growing Amanda noticed that Kimberly was trying to pick a fight with Maya by punching her arm with her fist while Maya was driving up hills on the narrow and steep bumpy pothole roads, and for a short time Amanda feared for her life. The two other women in the back seat next to Amanda didn't pay any attention to the drama in front of their eyes. They were comparing messages on their cellphones and laughing and making obscene comments. "*Possessiveness. Entitlements. Jealousy. Imbecility. The downside of love,*" Amanda thought. "*The real cost. And the upside of love? Any? Think! Think! Concentrate! Children.*"

After a long scary ride that seemed to last forever Maya parked the car on top of a mountain with a great view of the sea in all directions. The women decided to have the picnic on a nice spot at a cliff overlooking the sea. Felicia defiantly insisted that she was carsick and not hung over and then immediately threw up just outside the car. She missed spraying the car by an inch but managed to hit her white sneakers and add a greenish hue.

Kimberly laughed and made a sarcastic comment about alcoholics and poor suckers not being able to hold their liquor and called Felicia a *slob,* and suddenly there was a heated discussion going on about relationships and ownership and patriarchy and norms and the establishment and double standards.

"*Open relationship*, my ass!" said Felicia. "Just an excuse for having your cake and eat it, Kimberly!"

Greta turned to Amanda who didn't want to get involved in the discussion, and said:

"Amanda. You're straight, aren't you? What's your take on this?"

"*None of your fucking business!*" Said new Amanda-voice in her head. Amanda was silent. She just smiled.

Greta smiled back and gave Amanda an evaluating, curious look while she opened the first wine bottle.

"No labels, Greta!" said Maya. "Please! Just leave her alone, will you!"

"Oh come on! You *do* look straight, lady. Straight and reliable. *Matronly*," said Greta with a deep throaty voice. For some reason Kimberly found this very amusing. She couldn't stop laughing.

Amanda touched the white stone in her pocket and didn't reply. She just smiled.

"You look *great!*" said Maya, so silently that it might just have been a figment of Amanda's imagination, or maybe the stone speaking. But Maya's lips *were* moving and she *was* looking at Amanda.

Greta, Kimberly and Felicia stripped off their clothes and went for a nude swim further down on the deserted beach and Maya and Amanda stayed to keep an eye on the food and piles of clothes and boots and empty wine bottles and purses filled with all kinds of valuable trash like credit cards, cigarettes and cell phones.

"*We are the Guardians of Earthly Possessions,*" whispered the stone in Amanda's hand.

Amanda and Maya were silent for a while. Then, out of the blue, Maya said:

"We are breaking up, you know. I can't deal with the constant fighting and her fits of anger and mood swings and constant infidelity any longer. I just realized I've had enough."

"Oh, but that's *so sad!*" said Amanda.

"Is it, Amanda?" said Maya. "Really? *Sad?*"

Amanda blushed as if Maya could read her mind. Then again, Amanda had never had a poker face.

"Well, perhaps it *is* a bit sad after all," said Maya. "Our sex life was always hot. Angry sex. Makeup sex, breakup sex, well you know? *Hot-hot-hot.*"

"*Hot?*"

"You know what I mean! Accumulated anger. No restraints. Violent. Sizzling!"

"Of course. I know. *Passionate.*"

It was the third lie she had produced in less than a few hours.

Amanda had no clue as to what Maya meant, herself being an expert on tepid, infrequent and unpleasant sex only.

"Kimberly is a very mean person. Very, very insecure and manipulative. I found it attractive once. Lots of people do. *Lots!*"

"Yes! And she also happens to be very beautiful. In case you haven't noticed," said Amanda.

"Well, beautiful or not—she is toxic," said Maya. "Toxic people are fascinating. For a while. Until you are completely drained. They use up all your good energy and replace it with bad. And you get addicted to it. That's the worst part."

"I know," said Amanda and this time she wasn't lying. Actually she did know this from first hand experience: "They'll reduce you to nothing and you get used to it."

"Yes," said Maya. "Yes. I know what you mean." Their eyes met and Amanda started to feel faint and she sighed: "In the end you are nothing, feel nothing, you have shrunk, disappeared into a dark hole, distorted and lost...*like Alice...*"

"Are you feeling okay?" asked Maya softly, somewhere very far away in a fog in a parallel universe of love and kindness. And all Amanda could think of what how Maya had looked the day before, making love on the beach, her naked body, her hands, breasts, legs, all the of the miracle of her being. The image of Maya was mixed up with other, long forgotten images and repressed memories so strange they could have belonged to someone else, but she knew they didn't.

The toxic insects were buzzing in her head and in her heart and in her guts now, and she could taste the taste of blood in her mouth and feel a pounding in her head as if it was going to explode and a pain in her heart like a stab wound; and when the pain was so great that she could no longer breathe, or move and believed that she might actually die from the pain and the lack of oxygen and the lack of love—she fainted.

She regained consciousness after a little while and discovered that she was lying on the ground with her head in Maya's lap and that Maya was caressing her head.

"You passed out! I was going on and on about toxic relationships and you passed out. I'm so, so sorry, Amanda! I had no clue!"

But Amanda wasn't sorry. She was close to Maya who was very careful not to offend her by too imposing too much unwanted intimacy. But Amanda needed intimacy more than anything. She tried to support herself on her arms but fell back into Maya's lap, still lost and dizzy.

"Do you need anything? Water?" said Maya. "Tell me!"

So, still faint and with an aching heart, she looked Maya in the eyes and said, with a voice that was completely new, and completely her own:

"Yes I do need something. I love you. And if you don't kiss me now I will die!"

Maya smiled back at her.

"Well, we can't allow that to happen, can we!" she said and the sudden passion in her eyes made Amanda's blood sing.

⌇

Later that night they made love for the second time in the big oak bed in Amanda's room with the pale white moon as their only witness.

"I love you, too," said Maya. "I have loved you ever since I saw you with that sweet little dog yesterday. I don't know how any of this is possible, but you know; when I asked her to bring you the stone—she did!"

"But…? Was that *you*?"

"Yes! I wanted an excuse to get to know you. So I exploited an innocent, trusting dog."

Amanda was silent.

"Are you appalled? Please say no!"

"*Destiny…*" said Amanda dreamily.

"Destiny?"

"Yes! In the restaurant; how could you possibly have known that I would forget the stone on the table?"

"I didn't! I had my friend Johan the waiter grab the stone while you were admiring the beautiful sunset. You were quite lost in dreams there for a while! A true romantic!"

Amanda felt she had to make a confession, too.

"You know: I watched you making love."

Maya laughed.

"Yes, I *know*!"

"You do?"

"Yes! Let's hope the photos turn out nice!"

Amanda couldn't say anything because she was so embarrassed.

"Don't blush! Kiss me, *Precious*!" said Maya. "And let's adopt Destiny, the Dog!"

~

And so they did.

After all it was Destiny that brought them together.

~

~THE END ~

~

MayBe—A Pirate

Somebody once told me you should be careful what you are praying for. But I didn't know that night. The only thing I knew for sure that dark night, kneeling on the cabin floor, on a passenger ship in the middle of an ocean, crying my eyes out, was that I didn't want to get married to Mr. Southerby.

It wasn't just the fact that Mr. Southerby was more than twice my age, and ugly, he was mean too, in a hard, sophisticated, smug way that made me feel stupid as soon as I opened my mouth and expressed my opinions. I read a lot and I am well informed and like to exchange opinions. I had so many then and I have even more today.

I knew he despised women and being one, he despised me. Being clever he despised me more than he despised most women.

He did however, like my family name, and my genealogy, and the endless doors a name like mine would open for him was it to be attached to his own.

And my father had a similar taste for money. I had always known, of course, that I had to get married one day, because if I didn't I would end up an old spinster, like my Aunt Sally who got crazy and jumped into the ocean in the middle of the night, and whose body was never found.

I had never met her but whenever Aunt Sally was mentioned, which was very rare, my ears were always hot with attention. Apparently she had been a woman with a mind of her own. So my choices between marrying a horrible man and throwing myself into the ocean left me overwhelmed with sadness and I prayed to the skies and the moon above, tears rolling down my cheeks.

"Please take me away! Please, please take me away from here!" I prayed to the Universe.

Hardly had the prayer left my mouth before the door to my cabin was kicked in and a big man with horrible rough clothes stormed into my cabin and threw me over his shoulder and carried me away. My Nanny used to say I was spoiled rotten and always got what I wanted and maybe she were right. But the thought that I always got what I wanted didn't occur to me at the time hanging over the shoulder of the rough man like a sack of potatoes. I didn't see it that way. Not at the time it happened. At that particular time I was just afraid.

"Is this yours?" the man asked and nodded to a black suitcase in the corner of my cabin.

I let out a sound, or a sob, or a sigh, and he grabbed my heavy suitcase, too. Outside the door a young boy about my own age was waiting, and the man who was carrying me over his shoulder, put down the suitcase for a second and handed over an envelope to the boy and told him:

"Deliver this to the old gentleman with a beard who is tied to the piano upstairs! And return to the boat afterwards. We are leaving as soon as the men have collected the jewelry and money."

"Can I have some coffee beans for my mother?" asked the young man.

"Ask the Captain!"

The young man ran away in the corridor and I watched him disappear. If the rest of the passengers were tied up and about to get mugged, there was no way for me to escape. So this was the end, my fate, my destiny.

"Soon these brutes will rape me and probably murder me, but at least I won't have to marry Mr. Southerby," I thought, trying to keep my spirits high.

Then I must have fainted. (I seriously doubt I feel asleep.)

Yes, admit that I fainted.

To my defense I must add that I did so because I was a lady at the time and brought up to do so when being opinionated would be out of place and fainting would be considered ladylike.

I was also starved sad and bored to bits and slightly seasick too for that matter. Not that it matters.

Fainting was the appropriate thing to do but actually and for once when I didn't care I did the appropriate thing, just like that.

I was carried down a rope ladder into a small boat and placed next to all kinds of goods. When I opened my eyes again I realized that I had been the only living thing to have been taken from the ship. I just didn't how to look at this fact from my perspective? Was it flattering to be found so irresistible among irresistible ladies that I was the one they couldn't leave behind?

Or should I consider it a great insult to be placed next to a barrel of whisky, like a piece of property? The moon was shining white and round on a dark blue background above the dark blue ocean.

The moon was still smiling at me a few hours later when I was brought aboard a tiny ship with a strange black flag with a skull and crossed bones. My friend Eileen Von Ruben had shared some information with me about that particular flag and its symbolism. It was a pirate flag and it had a name.

"*Am I supposed to thank you?*" I asked the moon. "*Can I please make another wish?*"
A voice inside my head replied: "*Nobody can save you now. You will not survive the night aboard a ship with pirates. Remember the potion in the little brown bottle your mother gave you? The drug she told you to sip before the wedding night? Drink it all! You have no choices left now. Remember your Aunt Sally? You are finally about to meet her.*"

So when I was locked inside a small cabin along with the black leather suitcase I started to ransack it in search of the bottle with the potion. A small lantern provided some light and at first I was slightly confused. Until it dawned on me that the black suitcase was not my own suitcase, but my father's, and that there must have been a mix up.

Inside my father's suitcase were documents and some coins of gold, and some gentleman's clothing and a golden watch. There were also some horrid drawings of naked ladies and men performing horrid acts, hidden between the clothes. I wondered who had put such horrid things in my father's suitcase and for what purposes. Then the thought of my father opening his suitcase and having to face ladies' clothing and how that would be a far more severe chock to him than having his daughter abducted.

It was a mean thought but even so it made me smile, because, after all he had arranged the marriage without even considering asking me about my opinion in the matter. This was a small revenge. I thanked the moon. Who else could I thank?

When I looked through the deeds and read some of the conditions stated in the documents, I realized how I, by accepting to marry his business partner, would make my father an even richer man. So why on earth had he kept telling me that girls were of no use and worthless and nothing but trouble? According to these documents I was worth a fortune.

The sea was calm and men were singing and drinking outside the cabin. One of the men had such a lovely voice it made my eyes mist up again. I wondered how such brutal creatures could sing so beautifully about matters of the heart.

But then I remembered that there were birds that could speak the human language and not understand a single word. They sung sad songs about love and funny songs about fights and songs about the sea and when they sang songs about their mothers some of them cried. I had never heard a man crying before in my entire life and it was a very strange experience. I heard their voices through the thin walls talking about how they missed their mothers, in between gulping some alcoholic beverage.

I thought about my own mother. Did I miss her, I wondered.

Did she miss me?

Did she cry when she thought about my fate?

Did she cry when she thought about all her lost jewelry?

"They will come for me," I thought. "They will save me. I am their daughter. They love me."

But deep inside my heart I knew they didn't love me. They never had.

The songs outside my cabin were so sad. They were all about love, now.

I didn't want to get married to that mean old man.

I tried to cheer myself up and I thought about how me being abducted and killed by bloodthirsty pirates would impress my silly friends. There was something both dignified and horrible at the same time about my fate and they would turn me into a legend of sorts. Evelyn Mc Naughtbright might think about me at night and sigh to herself. This thought was slightly comforting.

"Poor, poor Maya!" Evelyn would sigh to her chamber maid

who would be combing her long hair before going to bed, while being bored to death and secretly envious of me. Maybe I would turn into a ghost and haunt them, all of them, all of my friends, after my death, and watch them with their ugly old husbands, while they were fantasizing about my horrible fate aboard a pirate ship. They would all be envious like crazy of course. I actually smiled when I envisioned this scene in my mind because I knew so well how their minds were working.

I was too afraid to sleep and decided against it, but must have dozed off despite my firm resolution not to. I woke up by somebody touching my arm lightly:

"The Captain wants to see you," a young male voice said.

So I did survive the night without any calming potion and I was brought to the Captain of the pirate ship like a guest of honor the next morning. Compared to the tiny cell I had been spending the insight inside this room was rather elegant and the furniture looted from the most elegant of interiors.

The Captain was standing at the end of a long polished mahogany table. A few lanterns lit the small space. He looked me over and frowned.

Then he opened his mouth and I realized he was a she.

"Sit down!" she said.

And I did. Usually I don't take orders from anyone, except my father of course, but I figured that this wasn't the proper time to stick to etiquette. And a Captain of a ship is after all still a Captain of a ship and me being just a lady was not an advantage at this point especially since the sea was getting a bit rough.

Maybe I was not even a lady any longer. I hadn't brushed my long hair since the day before and my wig must have fallen of my head into the sea when I was carried from the passenger ship. My long dress was getting dirty. The Captain wore her hair in a long ponytail like a pirate and she was dressed like a man in simple trousers and a white blouse.

"Can I offer you something?" she said.

"Why am I here? " I asked trying to keep a crumpet of dignity intact. By now I felt green in more ways than one.

"Why do you think you are here?" she said, a tint of curiousity in her voice.

"I don't know…"

Coarse laugher from the men working outside on the deck, making coarse jokes made me feel very faint.

"Well, let's not get lost in philosophical questions," she said and smiled for some reason. "We might never know why we are here."

"I am just relieved that I am still alive, Ma'am Captain…maybe not for long…"

"You are worth far more to us alive than dead."

I thought of the crew and the men working outside, laughing and cursing and spitting and felt faint.

"I see…" My voice was hardly audible.

"Your family knows where you are."

"They do?"

"Yes. We have informed them of your whereabouts. And we have informed your fiancée, too."

A black cat came walking over the table and she smiled and stroked the cat. Next moment a white parrot settled next to the cat.

"Aboard this ship we are all a family. All equals," she said and patted the cat. "This is Tim. He is thirteen years old. My baby. Nobody is equal to him in my eyes, though."

I started to laugh. "Family!" The thought was preposterous. Actually the whole situation was preposterous. But she was serious.

"Have a pear!" she said and pointed to a bowl with fresh fruit. "It will keep your legs straight."

I took a pear and it tasted lovely. I closed my eyes. It was absolutely delicious.

"*Family*?" I repeated, discreetly wiping off some pear juice from my chin.

"Yes. You have nothing to fear from the men when you are aboard this ship."

"I must confess I have heard differently…" I said.

"Of course you have "heard differently.""

She smiled at this too.

"Are you all…*pirates*?" I asked. "Real ones?"

"Of course we are. Genuine. Thoroughbreds."

It was her turn to laugh. I have not what my relatives refer to as a "poker face" so I feared she could read every emotion that went through my mind and body.

"We have a set of rules of conduct we live by. Etiquette as you might say in your world. And if you don't like those set of rules you are …out. The same rules apply in our world as in yours. The main difference is that we are decent. Your are not in your world. We only steal from the big thieves, not from starving women and men. We enjoy a good fair fight, between equals, not a brutal slaughter on the poor and innocent or defenseless human beings."

I don't know why she told me all these lies but perhaps it was to keep me calm or to persuade herself that she was a good person doing good deeds.

I suddenly remembered than among many of the truths my friends Frederica had overheard and later told me in confidence of course, one stated that pirates sometimes ate human flesh. And the flesh of young virgins was most sought after. It was some kind of pagan tradition they had developed a taste for and cultivated for centuries. I decided not to ask the Captain about this tradition (any particular dates or such) before I was certain of her plans concerning my future.

"You are our special guest until your father has paid the ransom for you. In the mean time there are some men aboard this vessel who would like to know how to read. So you might provide reading lessons."

"You cannot be serious? I am a lady!"

"I see. A lady! So would you prefer to take care of the animals? They are noble creatures, too. And very innocent."

"No!"

"Aboard this ship you work and you eat. And you eat and you work. Aboard this ship, guest or no guest, the same rules apply to all the members of this bark."

"I see. But do you have real books aboard?"

"Of course we have books! All kinds. Real ones, too. We collect books! Particularly books banned by some of the authorities we don't obey. Have your pick at the library!"

"Why would they want to learn how to read? They are ignorant…!"

I could tell my voice was filled with scorn but she didn't seem to care. All she did was to observe me closely for a second before she told me:

"Little Jim is the oldest son of Martha Smith; a widow with ten children, all under the age of fifteen. Her husband was murdered when people found out that their son was a pirate. Now Jim must to provide for his mother and little brothers and sisters. And not just financially. His most cherished dream; and he told me this once when he was sick and suffering from high fever; is to bring home of book of fairy tales with beautiful pictures and stories of fairies and elves and giants and dragons, and be able to read it to his younger siblings. He loves his little brothers and sisters more than you can imagine."

I frowned. It has not occurred to me that the pirates might have families. Nor had it occurred to me they might have room for any civilized emotions behind their hideous grins and enormous muscles.

"Jim fainted when they told him how the soldiers had tortured and slaughtered his father in front of his family, and how they had thrown the remains of his father's body to the hogs. He is a very sensitive young man, you know, cries a lot, even though he will be fifteen in January, but he the best fighter we have. Be kind to him. Don't read the cruelest fairy tales, whatever you do, or he might faint."

I was silent.

"Have another pear, girl!" she said finally. "We don't want you to starve to death."

Jim was a sweet young boy and very shy around me at first. When he had finished his chores on the ship he joined me in the cabin they referred to as the library which was incidentally the same cabin they kept the noble passengers Mr. Pig and the chicken Mi, Mo and Ma. Jim was very eager to learn to read. It was pure magic to him, putting letters together and building worlds in the process, and I accepted my responsibility. I also happened to feel very intelligent. But maybe it has something to do with the fact that Jim was extremely bright.

He told me about his family and we laughed a lot when we got comfortable together. He brought me some pears and I gave him my father's watch. We laughed so much that my stomach ached.

One day we were in the middle of a reading lesson, Jim, I, and Mr. Pig when a sudden noise interrupted the lesson.

"So they have come to rescue me," I thought. "That was quick! I can't wait to tell my friends about my adventure."

There was an awful fights going on the deck with swords and fists.

Jim and I watched the fight, fascinated and appalled at the same time.

Suddenly the Captain approached the fighting men. She was fearless as always, straight backed and tall and her voice was angry:

"I must ask you to leave my ship immediately!" I heard the Captain say.

"So you haven't changed your mind?" The bloody man said, panting still holding his fist up against poor Paul's face.

"Nope," she said. "Nor will I, ever."

"Cause I won't give up! EVER!" he shouted, grinning a big grin. Then he collected his men and left the vessel.

Jim and I returned to our reading lesson. We sat down at the table and he sighed.

"Mr. Bluebird again. He is the Captain of that other pirate ship you saw out there. He and the Captain used to be a couple back in the old days and then he drank too much and she kicked him out one stormy night.

"Kicked him out? Into the sea, you mean?"

"Yes. That's how she became the Captain of this ship. She kept the ship and looted some castles in France, and refurnished some of the cabins inside the vessel, being a lady at heart. And since she had been the one in charge most of the time and Mr. Bluebird was drunk most of the time, we decided to make her Captain. Once or twice a year he returns with his new ship and new crew to beg to be allowed to come back and when he can't return, he beats up a few of us just to show off a bit. He wasn't much of a fiancé in the old days when he was her fiancé and I think he likes it this way. It gives him a good reason to fight and drink and cry and sing songs of love to her. Now and then he brings some furniture. She likes that."

He interrupted himself.

"Why are you looking so sad all of a sudden?"

"I thought those people might have come for me, to help me return to …my folks…"

"You did? Seriously?"

"Yes!"

"But now when you have been hanging out with pirates you are no real lady anymore. To your folks I mean. I am sorry to offend you but I am just making a guess here. My father was killed because I became a pirate. In front of my little brothers and sisters. Then the soldiers burned down their house. Because of me."

"How do you know all this?"

"They make sure everybody knows what happens to those mixed up with pirates. In any way."

"No, I mean how did you know… about the rest? What took place in the village?"

"The flags. Pirate language. We signal with the flags. Like reading," he said and he sounded very proud and sad at the same time.

"You read flags? It's a language?"

"Yes, or a code rather. We belong to a country with no boarders. We are all part of this big family of pirates. We keep in touch!"

They were lovely once I got to know them. Once I got used to their smell. And my own.

"He won't pay," the Captain told me one evening.

"What?"

My head was spinning.

"Why?"

"The truth is, you are more worth to your father dead than alive."

"I see. And that means I have to…go!" I said, my eyes filling up with tears.

I watched the sea, the origin of all life, kind and brutal, ever changing force of life, but fair, equal, treating all living creatures equal. Just as she did, the Captain did.

"Your reputation is damaged. You have to leave your family."

"But I know things now! I've got skills! You need me, now! I am your teacher now! Please let me stay!"

I started to sob. I couldn't stop myself.

"Good!" she said. "Of course you must stay! Because this is your family. Put on some decent clothes now will you and get rid of that awful dress! And remember: No work, no food!"

"*Maybe…*" I sobbed.

And that's how I got my name.

My name is MayBe.

Before that my name was simply May.

Long story.

So maybe it is. And maybe it isn't.

MayBe.

I wanted to become a lady.

Instead I became a pirate.

Long story.

You could say it all started when I was sold like a piece of property.

I cried a lot at the time.

I cried about the loss of the loved ones I called my family. Aren't you supposed to?

Even if you don't love them?

They weren't really my family and they didn't really love me, but I didn't know at the time.

Or maybe I knew and didn't want to know I knew all the time.

It takes a long time to know oneself.

Who you really are.

I am twenty-two years old now and I am still surprised at all the things I learn every day aboard this ship.

I thought I was a lady, and that I was going to marry my father's business partner and that I would become wealthy and wear beautiful dresses and go to balls and society functions and feel miserable most of the time.

I had never spat on a floor before or dressed in men's clothes. Now I do and I love it. I climb the ropes and love it. I have developed some nice muscles and I am strong as a young horse and I love it. I look like a young man and feel like a young woman and I love that, too.

I speak up and they listen. Everybody speak and listen aboard. Those are the rules. They call it democracy. I always believed democracy was a club of sorts for old white men with lots of money, but here everybody has a piece of democracy, so even I count.

I didn't want to get married to that old fart. I never wanted to get married to anyone for that matter. I am like my Aunt Sally who is the Captain of this ship, because she didn't drown that time. But that is a completely different story.

I like wearing trousers. It is easy to work in. I like to get dirty and sweaty and curse and spit. I was never allowed to do these things before, since I was brought up to be sold to a man in exchange for some important property. *Quid pro quo* as the lawyers say.

I don't know my father very well but according to Aunt Sally he is the human incarnation of the Devil himself. But maybe she exaggerates just a little.

Still the men are kind to me. I don't understand it. I was brought up to believe that that the apple is as bad or good the tree it grew on. That would make me part Devil too. But they look at family and what makes a family a family, in a different way from what I was used to. So do I these days.

They say that I am not my father. That I am responsible for my own actions only. They don't accept cruelty for the sake of cruelty. And nobody is richer than anybody else. Their ways of looking at things make my head spin sometimes. But it spins in a nice way and I hope it won't stop spinning.

I keep getting these new thoughts all the time; thoughts about the world and men and women and justice and muscles. I love mine. My thoughts and my muscles that is. They aren't new. They were always there; I couldn't see them or hear them, that's all.

We split everything aboard. Even I get my share of goods and looting. I still have a weak spot for jewelry to be honest. Emeralds and rubies. So lovely. My brother Jim loves them too.

The people I feared and hated are my family now, and the ones I used to call my family are my enemies. Strange? Not really. Family is just a word. So is loyalty.

I learn more things about friendship and loyalty and courage every day.

They are the kindest people in the world, once you get to know them. But that might take a while. And you have to get used to the language of course.

I feared for my life once, and for my virtue.

But pirates don't fear anything. They are fearless, because they are truly good people.

Back home they would not dare to leave me alone in a room with a strange man. My reputation might be blemished. Here I work with men every hour of the day and we sleep in the same place, and sometimes we fall asleep on the deck too exhausted to move, but nobody has ever touched me inappropriately. I am part of their family now. We are one body. We are family. One family.

I think I am starting to fear civilization more than anything. Civilization made me into a pretty doll that was put on a shelf.

My father sold me to his old business partner.

I can't ever forgive him. Or my mother.

☾

We are striking at night at 12 hours. It will be my first. I am so excited!

The moon is high and I blow her a kiss. My family smile. They like the little feminine streak in me.

They are kind. They only want justice.

For me it is personal.

Tonight I will get my revenge.

My name is MayBe. See you in your worst nightmares?

...Maybe?

❧The End❧

A Frame for the Soul

That was the summer we spent talking about the weather.
It was great.
The weather, I mean, not the talking about it.
Well, you should do something meaningful with your life, and what is more important than the weather? When you think about it? So why not talk about it?
So, that's what we talked about that summer.
The impact of weather and stuff.

My father wanted me to sit for her. That's why I went there the first time. My father and my mother wanted her to paint a portrait of me. Like in the old days; oil colors, canvas, gilt frame and all that posh stuff; museum and staircase old gothic castle style.

Stupid, if you ask me.

I mean for a tenth of the price and a tenth of the time you could have your picture taken at "Glamour Center". The people there make you up so you look a celebrity anyway you like it. And it is really nice.

Really realistic, too, of course because it's photography.

But, the old guy wanted to impress on his Mayflower gang, or his crowd in the Country Club, or the Yacht Club bunch, I guess.

And that's why all of this took three months instead of two hours.

And that's why.

That's why.

All of it.

∾

And this artist. Well, I took a yellow cab to her studio, which was not in the chicest part of this city, if you know what I mean! And later she told me she wanted to capture my soul.

Well, well! There was ambition if I ever saw it! Or black magic! Who knows? Really?

She said my makeup was on the heavy side, and so was my clothing.

I was thinking that *she* was on the heavy side. But I didn't say so. I just blinked with my blood red mouth, my false eyelashes and smiled sweetly with my blood red mouth.

So she met me downstairs in this old brick building in the meat district and we went into her studio, which was on the top floor. Very good exercise climbing all those stairs, if you ask me!

It smelled strange in her studio—but not at all unpleasant— of oil colors, turpentine, linseed oil, coffee, sweat, wood.
I was thinking that it smelled old.
An artisan smell. Time travel smell.

The artist woman had put some posters on the brick walls and I had a closer look at one of them, as I passed by.

It was an old black and white photograph of a wooden armchair with leather straps attached to it, everywhere. A name was printed on the bottom of the poster: "*Amnesty International*". I had never heard of them, but I thought I might try out their next album. Cool picture, cool name, too!

Used brushes of all sizes were drying in tin jars and glass bottles all over the place, leaking tubes of oil colour lay on small tables, pieces of torn cloth lay on the floorboards, framed canvases were leaning to the red brick walls, sketches, sketches everywhere, pencils, a ladder, small chairs, cardboard boxes, empty wine bottles, same with red candles in them. There were color stains everywhere, even on her clothes.

The sun was shining down on the floor through the multitude

of windowpanes in the skylight window, and the shadows made sharp black lines on the white naked floorboards. Neat, if you ask me! The place had potential. Even though the place was a bit sloppy—for an old person, I mean!

So I sat down in an armchair in the middle of the room and studied my new black leather boots through a lock of my curly black hair that hung down in my face over one eye.

Oddly enough, the purple velvet armchair went well with my black leather outfit. Neat! I felt in control. Cool.

"I want to paint the real you!" said the artist woman. "The essence of you. Who you really are. It might take me a while to see it, so let´s talk for a while and I'll I'll make some sketches of you! Relax! Just be yourself!"

Well, who the fuck else could I be! I thought that was such a weird and artsy fartsy thing to say to a kid.

What could I do in that situation? I started to talk about the weather, like my parents always do when they feel uncomfortable or run into idiots or poor people or old boring farts with two brain cells :

"The weather is nice today!" I said in my most polite and pleasant schoolgirl voice.

She stared at me behind her ugly prescription glasses as if she was surprised. But, I mean, what else do people talk about when they don't know each other? The Dow Jones index?

"Do you think so?" she asked. "Why?"

"*Why?*"

She asked me why!

"Why *what*?"

"Why do you think the weather is nice?"

She started to sketch on a big sheet of paper with a thick pencil.

"Oh...? It's beach weather! Sunshine! Warmth, you know!"

"What about skin cancer?" she asked.

"Yeah. You are right. Of course. But I take care of my skin".

"I see. How?"

"How *what*? Oh! Sun factor sixty."

"Aha!"

Then she was silent. I tried to think of something to say. I was trying to figure out why she asked me such a weird question. This never happened to my parents. She wasn't trying to put me down or anything. No, not that stuff. And she wasn't acting superior either. She was just... well... *observing* me.

"Well. I do like rain, too," I said.

"You do?" She did sound a bit impressed, actually, but she didn't ask me why, this time though. So I told her, anyway.

"....because it' s nice being indoors when its raining."

"Are you a house cat?"

"No, I m not a cat! I happen to be a very human being."

She laughed, so she did have some sense of humor.

"So, what do you do when you stay indoors?"

She put her pencil up in the air.

"What I do? Well.... people do? I mean. Watch TV, I guess."

"Aha, so you don't watch the rain?"

I couldn't answer that one for a while.

"No, not while I'm watching TV," I said finally. (Smartass!)

"Touché!" she said. (Some technical term for sticking the pencil up in the air, like that, I guess.)

"Yeah. Touché," I replied. Whatever the fuck that meant.

We sat silent for a while. I watched her drawing me on that sketchpad. Quick movements over the white surface, like tics.

"Do you like to read, Melinda?" she asked.

"Well, there is this book you can buy with all the serial killers in it."

"Did you read it?"

"No, I don't read much, so I won't buy it. But it is very popular, a bestseller. You get all the details of the murders, and all the names of the victims, too. But people only remember the serial killers. It's not cool to be a victim."

"I guess not," she said.

"You know, I have always wondered how they know which one to kill? Really! I mean, like I didn't even I know what channel to watch on TV last night!"

"So what did you finally decide?"

"I decided to watch a film about a woman who killed somebody who raped her when she was a child. There was a lot of blood in the film. Well, not real blood of course! Or, maybe it was real blood, after all?"

"Do you think so?"

"Who cares, anyway?"

She didn't reply so I continued talking. I like to talk.

"Did you know that the human body contains more than one gallon of blood? And a lot of other stuff also, of course. Yucky!"

"Yucky?"

"Yeah! And imagine that there are people around who eat people! Cannibals. Whatever for I don't know, because there are food stores all over the place, more than you care to remember."

"True."

"Well maybe those people are really, really poor? Or really, really hungry? Who cares? Really?"

"That's appalling!" she said.

"Well, there are lots of appalling people around, when you look. I look. I should go to Hollywood. People are beautiful there, all of them."

"Do you think so? Why?"

"Because they workout a lot and have good cosmetic surgeons there. Nobody has to look older than twenty-five. Unless they are poor, of course."

"Interesting theory!"

"Yes! Marilyn Monroe lived there, I think. Every man alive wanted to sleep with her. Even the gay ones. I don't believe she killed herself. No way. She had everything that really matters in life: beauty, fame and money."

"So?"

"I believe she was murdered. The Kennedy brothers thought she was getting too old and too fat and more famous than they. And then some people shot them too. I wonder why? It must be because of Marilyn Monroe."

"That's awful! Do you really believe that?"

"Yes! I do believe in personal revenge, I do. It's a good thing you can buy a gun if you need one, in this country! The world would be a better place if you could kill all the bad guys. Think about it! Only the good guys would be left!"

"Says who?"

"That's true! The tricky thing for a girl would be to ever get a date if she is good, and survive it if she is bad!"
The artist woman laughed at my comment.

"How old are you, Melinda?" she asked. "You think a lot, don't you?"

"I'm sixteen. But everybody thinks I'm older because I'm so mature for my age! I am a thinker, I am. I am a po-et, and I know-it! I am a smart-ass. Only I don't say "ass" in public. I am lady, you see! I don't say "shit", I say, "shoot". I never burp in public either. Only when I'm pissed. Who cares anyway?"

"Some people care."

"And you, how old are you? And what's your first name, by the way?"

"I'm Vendela. My artist name is Vendela W. I'm thirty-five. And as for my own mind, I can only say that I have just started to understand a few things."

"Poor you! I hope I'll understand more than a few things when I'm that old!"

"Who knows? We all make mistakes and some of us pay for them."
She smiled at me but it wasn't exactly a friendly smile.

She wore no lipstick and very little mascara. Her dyed, not permed, not cut, not curled, just plaited in a long pigtail in some kind of boring blonde shade, similar to my own boring natural hair colour, actually, as I recall it, many, many hair dyes ago. Her clothes were boring, too. She wore a knitted blue baggy sweater over plain blue jeans. Her shoes were worn out.

Boring, all of her, if you ask me.

I mean, you do expect an artist to be crazy, I mean, that's the package deal! Weird clothes, crazy hairdo. You do need to show people that you know what you are doing; that you can't help being so different and cool; it's in your frigging DNA; I mean, how else do you expect people to know you have talents? But maybe this old lady had no real talent?

Maybe she just slept with the right people, ages ago?

Who knows?

Who cares?

"Well, do you like snow, Melinda?" She asked after a few minutes. She was drawing and I was getting bored for real, now.

"Sure. We go to Aspen every year, the whole family. It's awesome. You meet a lot of interesting people, there. Rich and famous people. You make connections."

"Do you ski?"

"Of course! You have to. Hated it when I was a kid but I had a very good ski instructor. The best."

"I bet."

"I'm very fit, you know. If you were a guy I could show you how fit I am. I don't want to boast, but I have a great body, you know. Toned. Flexible."

"Yes I'm sure I would have liked to see it if I were a guy; or a photographer, for that matter. But, now I'm painting a portrait of you; I'm not working for *Sports Illustrated.*

"Well, let me put it this way:" I said to her: "You can't have it all!"

Actually, she looked a bit angry. He! He! Sore spot there, no doubt!

Was she to poor to afford a Hasselblad, or dark room equipment? Anyone can take a picture, so that couldn't be the problem; it takes no talent to press a button.

Well, artists are supposed to be poor. It's good for them to starve a little. Makes them work better. Somehow I started to think of the story about the donkey and the carrot. But instead of the donkey, there was this artist woman running after the carrot. So, I giggled.

"What's so funny?" she asked me.

"Oh. Nothing. I was thinking of a carrot, that's all."

"A... *carrot?*"

"Yeah. I am a bit crazy, you know. Ask my friends. Well, anyway, how much does my father pay you for this stuff?"

"This...*stuff!* What *stuff?*"

"For painting my soul?"

"Why don't you ask him?"

"Who cares?"

"Yes. Who cares," she repeated in a slow voice.

Then she went to a corner of the room and picked up a huge white framed canvas on an easel. I could hear her draw lines on the white surface with small sticks of charcoal. I could hear her scratchy sounds. Like a cat's claws.

"Do you like painting?" I asked her.

"It happens."

"I also liked to draw and paint when I was little but, you know, you got to have a real job, so I don't do it much nowadays.

"Well maybe its better that way."'

"I was really good, you know. Seriously!"

"I bet. Did you have a drawing instructor when you were little?"

"No. Of course not! Waste of money. Mrs. Jonson, my teacher, called me a child prodigy, whatever that means."

"I see!"

"But she was a wacko! Nagging about my *talent* all the time." She kept drawing and sweeping the canvas with short strokes with a cotton cloth. When she looked at me it was like I was a chair or something. So much for my soul.

"How much do you pay for this place?" I asked after listening to that scratchy sound for a while.

"Too much!"

"What do you mean; too much?"

"More than it's worth."

"How much is it worth then, in your opinion?"

"It's just a place where I work. It' s space. How much is space worth? What do you think? How much is *space* worth?"

"I don't know."

"Well, I don't know, either!"

"Well, you know; I didn't ask how much space was worth, I

think I asked how much you pay in rent, didn't I?

"Oh, I see. Can you lift your head a bit please!"

And she looked at me again like I was some kind of a vase with a flower, or some *thing*.

"Don't look so angry, Melinda!"

"Maybe it's not me! Maybe it's my soul that's angry!"

I think that got to her. Sometimes I am quicker than Superman. Anyway, she smiled at me and asked:

"What do you watch on TV, when it's raining?"

But she didn't sound too curious, though.

"I like realistic stuff. Like in real life, you know!"

"Aha. You mean films about being about being unemployed and poor, or films about being abandoned when you are a pregnant teenager with no money and no place to go, or films about how it feels to live out on the streets because your Mom is a drug addict, or films about being disabled, or sick or depressed?"

"What cable net are you on?" I asked.

"I'm sorry. It was a long time since I watched TV."

"Well if you don't watch TV; then how do you know what stuff to buy?"

She didn't say anything for a while, just coughed a little (but it didn't sound contagious). She was working behind the easel, and the only thing I could see was the huge canvas and five legs. I preferred the wooden legs.

"But how do *you* know what stuff to buy if you watch TV?" she asked after a little while. "I mean: How do you know what you really need?" .

I didn't answer.

What I really need?

Who cares?

Really?

When we had been silent for a while I asked her:

"What do you do if you don't watch TV? Do you paint all the time? To pay the rent, I mean?"

"No. I don't paint all of the time. And I don't always paint portraits when I paint."

"Well, I guess you meet a lot of interesting people when you paint portraits?"

"Absolutely. I can't deny that!"

"Like me," I said. (Why be modest?)

She threw her head back and laughed a loud warm laugh, like she thought I was joking.

Well, who cares?

"Would you care for a cup of coffee?" she asked.

"Oh no thanks! Coffee is bad for you!"

"Well, so is life! What can I get you instead? Milk? Mineral water?"

"Pepsi, please! Diet. No calories!"

("A cigarette would be fine, too.")

"OK, I'll see what I can find in the old kitchen! I'll be back in just a few minutes. Feel free to look around!"

And then she went into a the small kitchen next to the studio and I could hear her grind coffee beans and tap water into a kettle and strike a match to lit the gas stove.

I rose from the purple velvet armchair and walked around in the room. There was a lot of space. I turned some of her canvases that were leaning to the red brick walls. Some were really big and heavy and had a special smell about them, which meant that they were wet. I learned that a bit late though. Shoot! The colors were nice though. I could tell she liked blue. Different shades of blue. Ugly bodies in motion like waves.

She returned from the   kitchen with a wooden tray in her hands. There were spots of color all over the wooden tray, which made it look trashy. It fit the place. There was a yellow enamel mug with hot coffee in it, and a Diet Pepsi, and same small square chocolate cookies on the tray. (1000-1500 calories).

    "Here you are! Well I could see that you were looking at my paintings. What do think?"

    "I can see you like to paint people."

    "Oh yes! I try to capture the actual moment of transcenden-ce from one state of being to another; the actual physical and emotional experience and expression of that *metamorphoses* or insight, or whatever; the moment when you are your body's reaction to your minds reaction to your body's reaction of all this *insight*, when you are a whole person moving on to another state of consciousness; Well, the process of living, or evolving, mentally, emotionally, artistically, you could say."

"So you don't paint any pretty pictures?"

"Not if I can help it! *No!*"

"If I were a painter I would definitely paint pretty pictures. But it is harder, isn't it?"

"Yes! The more authentic an artist—and person!— you are, the harder you will find it to paint pretty pictures!" she said.

I got the feeling she didn't agree with me, somehow. But anyway she must have realized that what I was had said was right because after a while when she had swallowed some of awful looking jet black coffee, she said:

"Maybe you are right, Melinda! Maybe when it all comes down to it, it's all about painting pretty pictures. That's where the money is, anyway!"

"Yeah! You see, people aren't stupid, you know! They want their money's worth!"

"So tell me: You want me to paint a *pretty picture* of you; is that what you want me to do, Melinda?"

"Sure I do! Drop that *soul* thing. Leave that to the church people. They will take care of my soul, trust me! But I guess I'll end up in Hell like the rest of my horrible, delinquent friends. He! He! He! Don't worry! Just kidding! My parents pay a shitload of money (pardon my French) to the church and to the Opera and to the Theatre and to Starving Artist and who knows what charity, so we are bound to go to Heaven."

I took a deep sip of Diet Pepsi and continued:

"Did you know that we belong to the First Church of the Sacred Blood? Well anyway: As long as you remember to regret your sins the minute before you die, it's green. You can do whatever you like and still make it, into Heaven! It's like a credit card. Jesus paid a long time ago."

"You're really a philosopher of a kind," said Vendela. "How are you using all your insight?"

"What do you mean *insight*?"

"What kind of a person do want to be? What ambitions do you have? I'm just curious, Melinda, that's all."

"Curious? Who isn't? But I guess I'll just have to become at least a lawyer or a doctor. Or they'll kill me! "

"Interesting jobs! You will be able to help a lot of people if you become a lawyer or a doctor!"

"Sure! There are a lot of rich people out there who want to become richer or more beautiful. That could be fun. Sure!"

"Or you could help those who are poor and helpless!"

"Oh, come on! How could they pay me? If they weren't stupid in the first place they wouldn't be poor and helpless, would they!"

The artist woman didn't say anything and I couldn't see the expression on her face, because she was busy again behind her canvas, all of a sudden. I guess she was impressed with all my insight. Pondering about what an interesting model she had got, no doubt. I felt like smoking a joint. Or two. Or to eat the rest of those small brown square chocolate cookies on the tray. Silly, silly, silly! One hundred sit-ups. One hour of workout. But Diet Pepsi isn't filling. But there aren't any calories in it either— just one!—to fill up those hungry fat cells. I wouldn't have liked to carry around all of *her* fat. What's wrong with being pretty?

"I suppose your parents aren't stupid, Melinda? Not like most people on the planet?"

"Why don't you ask their accountant? He could tell you a thing or two. Or a million, for that matter."

"And what do you think?"

"Think about *what*?"

"About your parents?"

"I don't *think* about them! What do you mean? What are you getting at! Talk show stuff! They are perfect. And normal! Why should I tell you! You are painting me, not them, aren't you?"

"Yes, I am. And if I paint you pretty, like you want me to paint you, it's unlikely I will ever get to paint them!"

"Well, let me put it this way; at least I'm not fat! Or poor! Or stupid!"

She looked at me again like I was steeling her space, or something:

"You really are a most observant girl, aren't you, Melinda? You do notice all the important things!"

"Well, maybe I'll just become a brain surgeon, or something."

"Maybe you will. But I'm sure there are other ways of influencing people's minds. Less drastic ways, you could say."

"Sure. I think a lot of things in life are a matter of will power, really. If not all things. If you want to be rich and famous and get a prime-time interview on TV, you can. There are always ways."

"*Ways?*"

"I saw something on TV some time ago about a guy with no talents, no intelligence, and no money. He listened to songs by a guy named John Lennon—who used to be famous—over and over again. "Working Class Hero", "Power to the People", "Give Peace a Chance", and "Happiness is a Warm Gun". Now he is famous, himself, because he shot John Lennon."

"Fame," she said. "A double-edged sword."

"A *gun*," I said.

"You could do something for me," she said.

"Like what?"

"You could tell me something about your parents. And about your siblings. It would help me see you clearer."

"I'm adopted," I said. "There's only me. I'm a bad investment." And I laughed at my own joke because I knew they were crazy about me. But she didn't laugh.

"Tell me something about who they are!"

"They are rich."

The artist gave me a strange look. Maybe she didn't like to be reminded of how poor she was, and how unsuccessful compared to my parents?

Well, join the club, lady!

"Do you know why she gave you up for adoption?"

"Who?"

"Your birth mother?"

"Who cares?"

She started to press out little dots of color on to her palette.

She wasn't angry.

But she was working very fast on the canvas with big strokes with her brush.

Ugly I guess.
Untalented.
Unwanted.

Green nose, red eyes, blue ears, baby pink clothes and all of that artsy fartsy stuff.

Who knows?
Who cares?
I wasn't the one who was paying her, was I?

It was getting dark outside. It was raining. I was sitting in the purple velvet armchair and watching the tiny drops of water that fell on the skylight windows above my head, like small bombs over Nazis in Germany!

That was the the first day of the rest of my life.
It was the summer we spent talking about the weather.

The End

→➤♦☙◄←

A Sense of Style

On my way to Mrs. Forester's bedroom I turn off the vacuum cleaner to wipe the sweat off my forehead. My head is aching because I didn't sleep well last night. Not because of my neighborhood, no—and I always keep a knife and can of pepper spray under my pillow, just in case—No, it's the dreams I don't trust.

I stop for a while just to look before I enter the room, like I always do. It's part of my daily ritual, the Zen of my insignificant existence.

Mrs. Forester's bedroom is like a treasure chamber filled with exquisite objects. This is what happens when fortune and excellent taste is translated into beauty. Translated back into money even the most insignificant item inside that room could pay my rent for a year, and when I stop to think about that, and let the injustice of it all sink in, a familiar feeling of rage and fatigue takes possession of me.

Maybe that's why I don't notice her at first.

Earlier this morning Mr. and Mrs. Forester had one of their violent arguments about his sexual indiscretions and now Mrs. Forester is studying her own naked body in the mirror, curiously, as if she was planning to auction it on eBay and has no clue as to what it's worth.

I remain standing there in the doorway for a while, watching her. No harm in watching from a safe distance, is there? I have to seek my pleasures where I can find them these days, now when I'm more alone and more broke than the guy begging for coins on the street corner.

Mrs. Forester looks like a little girl dressed up in a woman's body, standing there in front if the mirror and looking for her lost self, somewhere in there; looking for clues where there are none to be found.

Mrs. Forester is unhappy.

I recognize unhappy. I have tasted, breathed, lived unhappy for so many years, and believe me, Mrs. Forester is very unhappy.

At the Zenith of my own unhappiness, I had Cindy, and my drugs and I looked like trash. Mrs. Forester has her unfaithful millionaire husband and her social life, and unhappiness becomes her like a designer's dress.

I hate her and I love her more than I can say.

And no, it doesn't make any sense.

Mrs. Forester cups her small breasts in her hands to study the effect, talking to herself in the mirror like she is practicing talking to a lover.

I smile. As far as I know there are no signs of a lover. Mr. Forester wouldn't allow it, for one thing.

She shakes her head a little to observe the effect on her rich auburn hair. It bounces back, full and luscious, to the shoulders. She had it fixed yesterday at Salon Big H. and I just happen to know it cost more than a full year of boxing lessons at Gary's.

Mrs. Forester never looks me in they eyes when I perform my job, vacuum clean or dust, or swab her floors. I prefer to think that its not because she is rude beyond comprehension, but because of some visual impairment common to the very rich.

Sometimes when I miss my drugs, and can't sleep because of memories, bills, and fighting neighbors, I curse her name and I call her a fucking snob. But then again; how can somebody be a fucking snob when she never fucks? And probably doesn't even know how to?

I laugh at her and insult her behind her back when the fact is that I'm so much in love with her it hurts, and she doesn't even acknowledge my existence.

Now she pouts her lips, pretending that the mirror is her non-existent lover. Then she sighs and turns her back on herself. On her way to her antique four-poster bed she grabs the remote control and turns on the TV set, and the next instant sounds of moaning and fake orgasms fill the room.

I can't stand to watch those films.

Especially not that particular film.

∼

She lies down on her big bed, on the dark red satin sheets, among a sea of soft red pillows; clutching the remote control in her delicate, manicured hand, watching the film from a safe distance. The effect on me watching her, lying there, naked, is devastating. Suddenly something clicks in my mind and I loose all sense of self-preservation, propriety and respect, and I lock the heavy bedroom door behind me and approach the bed.

Mrs. Forester sees me and gives a gasp of surprise, but she doesn't scream as I expected her too. She just looks at me and says:

"How long have you been watching me?"

The air is full of strange unidentified emotions. There is no script.

We are both aware that she is naked and that I am not and that I am infinitely much stronger than she is.

There is strangeness to the sheer reality of her—now when she is not performing in my own private fantasy—a strangeness that is both sexy and the opposite of sexy; like putting on a pair of glasses and seeing things too sharply. Tiny imperfections that weren't present in my private fantasies now jump out in my face, but somehow those little imperfections only make her more real even more desirable.

Her body is extremely well maintained from weekly massages, strict diets and aerobic classes, but it's the look in her eyes makes my heart beat like crazy. She is leaning on her elbows; angry but amused, exposed and yet perfectly comfortable in her own nudity, watching me watching her, and as uncapable to hide her curiosity as I am.

"God, you are beautiful," I say.

"Leave my room immediately!"

She points at the door with her free hand.

I disobey her command and instead of moving away from her, I move closer, and sit down next to her on her bed.

I gently take the remote from her hand and press the off button and the screen turns black. My bad mood dissolves into thin air as quickly as it appeared, along with the exposed body parts and the sounds of the fake orgasms.

I too, will disappear.

Soon I will leave this house of indignity forever.

Soon, but not yet.

See, I am bad girl, a sad girl, a strong girl, and I know I am going straight to Hell.

But this time I will arrive there with a smile on my face.

I can sense some kind of excitement, or hesitation in her, as if she is testing me. Sleep deprivation and boxing lessons have made me strong, but also a little insane, and she feels it and responds to it. She turns her head away from my glance and we both know she's just acting.

I don't do drugs any longer but when I can't sleep I think of her. Only her. Who knows, maybe she can sense that too?

She finally turns her head and looks me in the eye. It's the first time ever. Her pupils are dark and dilated and she is trying to conceal a triumphant smile.

"For three full months now I have wanted you to notice me," I say, my voice full of resentment.

"You have, have you...?"

"Yes. But you never did. Not once."

I tremble with repressed rage but she just smiles, as if she is amused.

"Imagine that!" she says. "Well, I notice you now. You have my undivided attention!"

My face is so close to hers I can smell the mouthwash and whisky of her breath when she informs me in a throaty voice:

"For your information: I'm not a lesbian."

I can't help but smile. With that look in her eyes who is she trying to convince; me or herself? She can't hide that she is attracted to me any more than I can hide my contempt for her arrogance.

"So what's this then, Mrs. Forester? Research?"

"None of your damn business! This is my house, I can watch whatever piece of trash I like without consulting my employees!"

"I guess it's your privilege."

She never looses her sense of style, not for a second—not even now in this awkward situation—and when she clears her throat and asks me some question she acts as confident and entitled as if she was conducting a formal interview in her stately office, wearing a business suit and not sitting in her unmade bed, wearing nothing but her birthday suit:

"Do you like what you are doing?" she asks.

"This, you mean?"

"Yes, this! *No!* Cleaning my house, of course!"

"You have no idea," I say. "Every day is a new beginning! And as a bonus I get to wear this lovely outfit!"

I lean toward her in my ugly baby blue polyester maid's uniform that makes me look like a joke inside a disaster.

"So do you enjoy scrubbing my floors? "

"There is nothing more satisfying in my mind than the prospect of getting rid of germs," I say, and my voice is completely calm and serious now, because I have finally regained my composure and I speak the truth and I know she knows it.

And she must have detected the shift in my demeanour and the sudden ominous calm in my voice, because the new situation makes her shudder involontary. I don't mind.

"Are you satisfied with my performance, Mrs. Forester?" I ask trying to meet her glance.

"Concerned. I must say you are full of surprises..."
I can't help laughing. She has no idea.

"Don't you ever get bored with your line of work?" she asks.

"How could I possibly? In a world like this, with endless opportunities for someone like me!"

"*Seize the moment*, you mean?" she says,"I agree. You really should. How do you think I ended up in a place like this?"
I put my hands around her neck and squeeze, and she just sits there with her ambiguous Mona Lisa smile.

"Go on, surprise me!" she says, still calm while looking straight into my eyes. I detect no fear or resentment, only excitement.

So I kiss her instead.

And when my tongue enters her mouth her entire body responds to the intimacy in a way that far exceeds my wildest night time fantasies. Words like *starving* and *drowning* comes to mind and I know that neither she nor I am safe anymore.
Then suddenly she catches her breath and whispers, pleadingly.

"Are you sleeping with my husband? Tell me now! I need to know!"
I can't help but laugh out loud at her preposterous question.

"Shit, no! Believe me; I have to be high to fuck a man. And I don't do drugs these days."

I can feel all the tension leave her body in her deep sigh of relief. Her fingers play with my short hair, comb it, and she touches my face with the sensitivity of a blind person.

"He is a monster, you know."

"I know."

My heart goes out to her. Everybody knows her husband is a monster, especially people like me. She continues to tell me about her marriage so I kiss her again to silence her because I can't bear to listen to it.

"I've been fantasizing about this," I say and inhale the lovely fragrance of her hair.

"It's you. Yes it's you," she says.

"Me?"

"In the movie."

∾

And yes, of course it's me. Making a fucking living, or a living; fucking, or whatever my confused mind labeled it at the time. But as it turned out Jimmy F.—the producer—was the one who was making a living—or making a fortune, actually—from that movie, while I, the star, lost everything and almost died.

It still doesn't make any sense to me, the unequal distribution of wealth and degradation; none of it does, but her words and the movie suddenly remind me of why I am still around, pretending to be alive when I'm almost dead.

And I wonder where *she* would she be without her unfaithful millionaire husband to boss her around and give her condescending looks and tell her how to sit and look and dress and act in his macho marriage script? Where would she be without all his money and the social priviliges that comes with it?

∾

"You are so beautiful, Serena. You have no idea!" she says and caresses my arms and my short hair. "Take off that hideous maid's uniform now, please! I can't stand to look at you, insulting your gorgeous body like that."

"So you know my name, Mrs. Forester?"

"Lucky guess, that's all."

Tenderly and slowly she helps me button up my baby blue polyester maid's uniform; lovingly, as if I am a gift from the goddesses wrapped in a hideous baby blue joke of a wrapping.

"Yes. It's you," she says.

"Come on! Seriously! There's no way you can tell after just a few minutes!"

"I've watched it ten times actually!"

"You have…? But why?"

"*Why*? It's so vulgar..."

"Yes! *And*... ?"

"*And*? Filthy. Disgusting. Violent. Degrading."

Every word feels like a slap in my face.

"Call it research if you like!" she says. "Or distraction."

I haven't felt this humiliated in a long, long time.

”Are you any good? Without a script, I mean?” she teases.

“What's your opinion, so far?” I ask.

“The kiss? Luscious!”

”I agree!”

“But the movie? Sublime!”

”It grossed a fortune. A monstruous succes.”

”Was that real? Or fake? That thing you did? You and that girl? ” she whispers in my ear, all of a sudden.

“I must warn you. It's dangerous territory!”

“Try me!”

“Dangerous for me! You know; excellence comes with a price tag, I am lethally good, and I paid for it with my body, my life.”

“Don't joke like that!” she says. ”No. No. Not funny!”

“True story, though. These are scars. Not ugly tattoos.”

She starts kissing my scars, killing me softly with her tenderness.

“*Mary Anne!*” I plead, helplessly. “*Please! Don't!*”

When I use her real name she hugs me so hard I can hardly breathe, as if she is drowning and I am her savior. As if she doesn't know it's the other way around.

∾

“Are you crying, love?” she says suddenly, stroking my hair.

I can't answer her because I can't speak. The most beautiful woman in the world is touching my scars, all of them, tenderly, one by one, kissing the coarse scar tissue close to my heart, caressing all my scars like they are the most beautiful things she has ever seen.

I can't get enough of her, the taste of her, the scent of her, and her touch makes my mind sings. I swim in soft sensations thick with emotions. And for a few precious moments she is mine.

I haven't cried since that time when I returned from Hell pretending to be alive, and now I can't stop myself.

And I don't know why.

This isn't working out the way I planned it.

Nobody is dead, nobody is leaving, but I am making love to the woman of my dreams and I am crying.

And I don't understand what happened.

≈

"Why the tears, baby?" she asks while she kisses the tears off my face in tender pecks.

"A big, tough girl like you?" she teases, while she traces the outlines of my biceps with her hand.

"Come on Mary Anne, you are a softie too!" I smile behind my tears.

"No. I'm certainly not!"

"Yes you are! After the fight with your husband you were so upset that you forgot to lock the door? Yes, *you*, Mrs. Mary Anne Forester; the embodiment of style and etiquette and pefection. Sloppy! Careless! Anyone could have seen you! Exploited you in so many different ways..."

She puts her index finger on my lips and smiles:

"Hush, hush. Forgot to lock the door! You're such an innocent at heart! Don't you have a mirror at home, gorgeous?"

~

She kisses me again, tenderly, and deliciously now, because now we are exhausted.

"I swear, the things a poor girl has to do to get laid these days!" she whispers in my ear.

"Yes," I say. "I couldn't agree more, Mrs. Forester."

~

—to be continued—

www.ingramcontent.com/pod-product-compliance
Lightning Source LLC
Chambersburg PA
CBHW061137200626
46817CB00016B/1835